The Core
Genesis

By Javonte Bostick and Johnny Hunter

DORRANCE PUBLISHING CO
EST. 1920
PITTSBURGH, PENNSYLVANIA 15238

Dorrance Publishing Co
585 Alpha Drive
Pittsburgh, PA 15238
Visit our website at *www.dorrancebookstore.com*

ISBN: 979-8-8872-9144-4
eISBN: 979-8-8872-9644-9

Chapter 1: Genesis

Every year has its dark days, but this bone-chilling evening particularly cries ominous. Dead in the autumn night, a dark figure slowly hones in on its target. Using the trees as cover, it awkwardly bends and twists its body in an almost unrecognizable shape as a means to further conceal its presence. Until now it's prey was carefully covering his tracks and meticulously outpacing the predator, but the sudden flutter of bat wings forced him to a halt. In the midst of the paranoia, the figure leaps into the air, pouncing on its target. SHNNNG! The sound of metal slices through the air, carrying a body along with it.

"Did you really think so little of me?" a voice calls out. Staring down at the blade running through him, then slowly gazing back up, the dark figure tilts its head in confusion at the smug-looking man before him.

"I honestly thought you were better than this," the man sighs as he throws a powerful front kick, sending the limp body soaring backwards. He carefully watches as the indistinct figure rises in the air, dissipating into the darkness. It was nothing but a mere silhouette, a shadow, an invisible foe. The man shakes his head and lowers his leg. Just before it hits the ground, his leg is grabbed and he's propelled forward with a slam. Now laying on his back, the man watches as a large shadow looms over as if to finish him off. Could it be the hostile from before? No. It was something similar but not quite. Standing over him was a spirited man with the exact same physique as his phantom nemesis. It was as if the shadow was mimicking this man, or rather the shadow was a manifestation of this man's own aura.

"There's only one word to describe me Kam: superior!" he says with a smirk. After returning a wry smile, Kam rises from the ground whilst perfectly executing a windmill kick. It looked like something straight out of a dance fighting scene. Following each spin, four small blades seemingly appearing from thin air are sent flying from his feet at an astonishing velocity. "Are you serious!?" the spirited man cries out as he casts a blanket of darkness in front of him to absorb the first two blades. Following that action, a pair of ghoulish hands emerge from the shadows to clasp the third blade, instantaneously sending it flying back towards Kam at break-neck speeds.

"Jace, you of all people should know that if I'm anything, I'm prepared," Kam says as he slightly jerks his head to the side, avoiding the returning blade.

Now kneeling on one knee, Jace winces, replying, "Well, if you're wondering what happened to that other nasty little knife, it was this close to having a dance party with my insides." As the showdown ends, a bombardment of lights come flooding in, illuminating the hunting grounds. Caught up in laughter, the boys barely even notice a third party approaching.   "You're lucky this is training, given there's usually a few freebies, but in the heart of the action when there's lives at stake, someone ALWAYS pays for their mistakes." The random voice echoing from the dark comes from a man who walks up to the two, wearing camo cargo pants, a black compression shirt, and combat boots. A sandy blonde-haired man with a sharp glare and a militant demeanor. Though you can say he has a mature look about him, in actuality he was just in his early twenties. He was Wade Holland: voice of reason, adoptive brother, lifelong friend. Speaking of which, dealing with those two often gave him the feeling of "having too much on his plate."

"Alright, bros, practice over," Wade emphasizes with a clap.

"Nah, really? What was your first clue? Me putting Jace down or us sitting here roasting marshmallows over a bonfire?" a sarcastic reply comes from Kam.

"Wait, whoa, where was I when that happened?!" Jace snaps back. When it comes to the story of Jace and Kam, it's hard to describe one brother without the other. They were like the dynamic duo you never knew you needed (because you didn't ask for one). The charming Kameron Scott and eccentric Jason Collins have always been like oil and water, but when it came to working together, they were more like fire and brimstone. The hellish combo have always had skills that complimented each other, no matter the subject. Sports, music, art, or combat, the teamwork between these two was sublime. If only that were the case for their attitudes towards each other. Without Wade one of them probably would've drowned in their own ego or started a secret new life in a third world country by now.

"Alright, guys, let's head back home before 21:00, we have to…" Bzzz ring! Ring! Ring! Bzzz Ring! Ring! Ring! The sudden outburst of chimes cause the boys to hastily search for their phones. They knew this sound could only mean one thing: Danger. The one who relays the message first is Wade.

"My crime alert app says that there's a major fire over at St. Katherines, it's gotta be those arsons again," he reports.

"The nursing home?! Why?"

"Dude, we know it's your app; you could've left that part out." Two deferring responses come from the boys.

"Well it doesn't matter now, let's suit up!" Wade asserts.

"Alright, but can we hurry this up?" Kam abruptly asks. "I kinda got somebody to see after this and I–"

"More important than this?!" Wade interjects.

"Bro, there's literally nothing more important than old people on fire. I doubt they can even stop, drop, and roll without slipping a disc," Jace says with a scowl.

"Okay, somehow that's even worse than what Kam said," Wade mutters while palming his face.

"I met this girl at Murphy's earlier and we hit it off. I was just hoping to see how it goes by the end of the night," Kam explains.

"And he strikes again," Jace chimes back in with a smirk.

"It's not like that this time. She might actually be the one," Kam replies in earnest. After the comedic exchange ends, the three-man vigilante squad heads for the crime scene. Arriving at the scene, the boys were immediately entranced by the roaring flames. Eerie sapphire embers enveloped the entire building, and if you looked closely, you can almost see the shape of a dragon glaring amidst the blaze. A brigade of firemen are desperately fighting to subdue the flames at every wing. Amongst the first response team is a large squad of policemen assisting in the search and rescue. In the center of the crowd, a sheriff is reporting in on the spiraling chaos. The account goes as follows.

"This is Sheriff Heinrich requesting back up for the code 10-72. So far there have been minimal casualties, but there are still some residents and staff unaccounted for. The prime suspects are confirmed to be the infamous Wake Sisters, who are still at large as of yet. There have been no signs of the flames dying down within the hour, which lead us to believe that supernatural forces are at work. I am requesting immediate back up, I repeat, requesting immediate…hold on, there seems to be three civilians approaching in odd clothing. Three males, one Caucasian and two African-American. They're all wearing some sort of high-grade protective gear and hero masks."

"Is that Kevlar? Wait, they're just a couple of kids…" the Sheriff mumbles to himself as the trio draws near. "Hey, you three, stop! This is a crime scene, DO NOT PROCEED. I REPEAT, DO NOT PRO–"

"I'm sorry, Sheriff Heinrich, did you say three masked men were approaching?" dispatch suddenly responds.

"HEINRICH! This is Chief Majors telling you to stand down! These men are more than capable of assisting us in the matter. Withdraw your men at once and leave it to them for the time being!" A drum-shattering voice can be heard through comms.

"But sir, they're just–"

"HEINRICH!" the chief interjects.

"Copy that," Sheriff Heinrich responds, snapping his head away from the radio. "All officers withdraw, I repeat, stand back!" The command is followed as instructed.

"I mean really…what type of sick bastard would incinerate a nursing home?" a voice complains.

"Well think about it, who doesn't hate their in-laws?" another voice responds in agreement.

"True, they really do rui–"

"Focus, guys! We got a job to do!" Wade angrily interrupts the foolish banter of the two boys. "Alright, so here's the plan," he begins to explain.

"Ah, there goes the catchphrase," Kam mutters to himself. With that the Hero Trinity springs into action.

"Alright, Kam, it's up to you to create something useful enough to smother the flames starting with all the exits. Once we figure that out, make slides and lifts and attach them to every window for a quicker escape route. Next send your soldiers inside to search for any remaining survivors."

"They're not soldiers, they're golems carefully crafted from–"

"Moving on…." Wade interrupts as he continues to explain. "Jace, deploy the phantoms to scout the area for any trace of the arsons. They'll act as surveillance while doubling as a safety net in case there's any lost or confused residents wandering around the grounds. If there's anybody left out there, it's your job to personally guide them back this way or apprehend them if they're responsible for all of this," he further explains.

"Huh? Grunt work again?" Jace openly complains.

"It's best if we let Kam handle the fire, the creatures you make could easily frighten the elderly, especially under these circumstances," a rational response comes from Wade. Kam snickers as he approaches the firemen.

"Ahem, gentleman, first of all, I want to thank you for all your efforts here tonight. From now on, I'll need your help attaching your hoses to the back of my golems. As you can see, their shape is akin to fire hydrants, with a rotating base in order to propel the water in every direction like a high-powered sprinkler," Kam discloses. As he says this, six stone-like figures slowly emerge from the ground. They all appear with heads resembling ancient Olmec statues, with the first two having four ducts protruding from where limbs should be. These hollow-eyed golems are exactly as described. The remaining four golems take on a more humanoid form, with two manning the hoses waiting to pull the lever.

"The remaining two will scour the building to make sure it's all clear. I pray there are no more casualties," Kam says with his hands joined together. With the snap of a finger, the cavalry advances. Meanwhile, leaning on the back of a squad car with his arms folded, there's a noticeably agitated Jace. With his hand cloaked in darkness, he scoops a small flame from the ground and watches it dance around his fingertips. The vivid black and blue contrast of colors waltz around this palms, the shadows dually acting as a guide for the flames and shield from the heat. He sighs in boredom as his ghastly wraiths return from the wreckage.

"Nothing to report, eh?" He casually converses with his crew, ignoring the glances up ahead. Right on cue, Kam turns from the group of firemen to sneak a joke in.

"Why don't you put on a puppet show for them or something," he jests while watching Jace twist his hands together, forming what seems to be a dog in the shadows of the flame.

Jace smirks, replying, "Since your Easter Island rejects are clearly doing all the work, why don't you just go play nurse with Wade over there?"

"He-he….he's just kidding, guys. I'm a doctor," Wade laughs nervously as he continues to examine the patients. At first glance, it seems like he's engaging in typical medical procedure, but the truth always lies deeper than the surface. Unbeknownst to the people, Wade Holland isn't your average man. With the slightest touch, he's granted the ability to peer into the vast memories a person contains.

"It's truly a blessing and a curse being able to scan through the innermost workings of the human psyche," he often says. After inspecting a few seniors, he comes across a woman whose look can only be described as absent. "I'm just gonna check your pulse and heart rate really quick, ma'am; is that okay?" he says reassuringly. No response from the senile woman before him. Now gently holding her hand, Wade suddenly feels a slight pinch. "Hmph?" He looks back up into the woman's lifeless gaze. Once again his hand is squeezed.

"I see…show me," he responds, diving into the woman's frail conscience. Carefully fast forwarding through the memories, glimpses of a painful past can be seen. A child abandoned by her parents at birth, a small girl cowering in the corner as her step-father unbuckles his trousers, a woman giving up hope on a world that has forsaken her. Holding back the flow of tears, Wade finally set his sights on a familiar place. Through the nursing home window, two figures can be seen bickering back and forth. A middle-aged Hispanic woman and her teenage daughter are responsible for the racket. The older woman walks around the perimeter dousing a can of gasoline around the building while screaming at the girl about how worthless she is.

"Dammit, Josie, see how far I gotta go just to make up for your incompetence?! It's pathetic that you even need a jumpstart for this. I can see why your grandmother abandoned you in the first place, you can't even take revenge on your own! You know how much I hate sweating, now look at me; I'm a mess! Since I gotta cover for your useless ass, we might as well kill them all while we're at it!" the woman yells with a crazed glare. The girl can't help but hang her head down, seemingly looking dejected.

She then takes a deep breath, smirking menacingly as she slowly lifts her head and whispers, "Alright, Stephanie, let's see if you can take this." In the blink of an eye, a dazzling sapphire flame arises as Josie sets the nursing home ablaze.

"Josie and Stephanie, Josie and Stephanie," Wade continues to recite the names of the assailants as he heads to the Sheriff to reveal the true identity of the Wake Sisters. Off in the distance, you can see Kam and Jace joining hands in triumph as the chaos subsides and the casualties were kept to a minimum. Another mission complete for The Hero Trinity.

*****

A man awakens in a poorly illuminated room.

"What the hell do they expect me to do now?" he says with a confused look on his face. Peering into the darkness, he notices something that would even raise the hairs on a lion's back. He wasn't alone. "What? No…..it wasn't…it wasn't supposed to be like this," he mumbles, frantically looking around the room at the countless pile of corpses. He's disheartened to see that his fellow comrades didn't make it. He grabs the arm of the body closest to him. No dog tags, no wristband, no form of identification. A John Doe. Appearing to have forgotten something important, he quickly looks down at his own wrist. He's relieved to see that his beloved watch is still with him.

"Huh?!" He suddenly blurts out. *11/10/2008, 12:31 P.M. it reads.* "That's impossible! How could two whole years have passed?!" he mutters to himself. Wondering how he's still alive, he scrambles around looking for any other survivors who can give him an answer. To his chagrin, the search was in vain. In the midst of his desperate ploy, he notices a reflection of a man in the metal operating tray. Shockingly enough he finds the reflection shown to be pieces reminiscent of the man he once was. What he had seen could barely be described as that of a man however. He had become something else entirely, and what he discovers next is absolutely mortifying. Dangling from his feet, there's a small piece of cardboard. He notices a single name on his toe.

"John…" He doesn't bother reading the rest of the name. A piercing howl reverberates throughout the room at such a powerful frequency it seemingly shakes the ground beneath his feet. While this can be said to be a considerably normal reaction, there was something unusual about this sound. It was the sound of 100 men and women all screaming for their lives. The bodies of the fallen were now positioned upright, screaming in unison as if they all shared the same pain. John's pain, John's voice, John's will.

Chapter 2: Uprising

It's a typical day at the Holland Estates. The gardeners are diligently trimming the hedges, the maids are dusting away to their hearts content, and the lovely Mrs. Holland is spending her Sunday making her famous soufflé. The man of the house is somewhere away on business wearing his usual gentle smile, for he knows his family is at peace. Or at least that's what he'd like to think. The involuntary twitching in the corner of his eye can't help but reveal his growing unease.

"What are they up to…"

"AH YEAH!" Ear-shattering music can be heard from the opposite end of the compound. This thunderous noise is resonating from a small single-story building that was carefully constructed for one purpose: discipline.

"Hm? At it again I see. These boys and their drills," Mrs. Holland mutters to herself as she cranks up the volume on her own radio.

"Ha ah!" Kam fires himself up as he charges straight for Wade.

"What's that supposed to be? Your fighting spirit?" Wade says with a furrowed brow. Noticing his increasing speed, Wade darts forward to counter the momentum of Kam's deadly rush. BOOM! The two boys clash forearms, sending a small shockwave throughout the room. "Tsk, tsk, all those black belts and trophies and you still haven't beaten me not once," Wade says boastfully. Kam flips backwards, retreating to regain ground.

"I honestly didn't want it to come to this. Once I unleash my Kam-Fu, all things come to an end," he says with an intense stare. Positioning himself on all fours like a wild boar, the usual spark in Kam's eyes disappears. This newfound glare seems to be emitting what can only be described as bloodlust.

"Wa-wa-wa-wait what? Did you just say Kam-Fu?!" Wade cackles uncontrollably as if this was the most absurd thing he's ever heard. With a mind devoid of all thought, Kam seizes the opportunity to attack. He starts with a rising palm heel strike, followed by a downward knife hand strike, but it's dodged gracefully. Falling face-first, he quickly catches himself with a handstand. In that same moment, Wade throws a spinning back kick, seemingly executing a perfect counter.

"Huh? No!" he cries out. Right before the kick lands, his foot is caught as Kam shifts his balance to one hand. At this point, it's clear who has the advantage. In that same position, Kam sends a barrage of kicks flying. Wade only manages to deflect the first few as he's sent soaring backwards with a bang. Now painted with a menacing expression, Wade rises in a slight stagger. "Che, I guess it's time to take the training wheels off," he grumbles as he walks towards a wall filled with various weapons.

"Welp, play times over!" Kam responds excitedly as he flips back on his feet. Now the real battle begins. Completely oblivious to the war zone back home, there's an overly ecstatic Jace making his way downtown.

"Loving just a little, touching just a little, oh, I'm losing just a little too much!" he belts out in a horrendous crescendo. Drawing near his destination, he notices that one of the more inconspicuous shops of the area is uncharacteristically crowded today. The bizarre atmosphere completely stops him in his tracks.

"Huh? Jay's Laundromat? I thought that was a dry-cleaning place. Oh, wait, same thing," he mumbles to himself, seeming to have come to a conclusion of his own. After walking down a few more blocks, he finally reaches his destination. In the middle of a plaza lies a locally renowned music shop: Murphy's Record and Tape.

"Yo, Murph, surprised to see me?" Jace calls out as he enters.

"Psh, please. I could hear your terrible singing all the way from Carol," Murph responds waving his hand down.

"You got what I need?"

"Yeah, just let me bag it up for you real quick."

"Good. You see I paid in advance. I told you I'm always good for it, Murphy."

"Why do you always say it like that? This ain't a drug deal, man," Murphy blurts out as the comedic exchange is cut short. "I'm sorry, but since you're so young, I just have to ask. I mean it's 2020, why do you always buy from here when you can just have a drone drop'em off at your doorstep or something?" Murphy asks while zipping his finger back and forth.

"Well, if you must know, I'm appealing to the nostalgia aesthetic," Jace answers almost immediately.

"Eh…the what?" Murphy replies with a troubled look.

"I don't know man, Kam told me to say it when people ask cuz it sounds cool. I should've known he was just messing with me," he says with his fists now clenched. The sudden ringing of bells causes the two to turn their attention towards the prestigious man walking through the door. In that same moment, scattered whispers can be heard all throughout the store. "Yes, yes, it's me, oh no, please don't faint," he says in a pretentious tone. It seems a celebrity has entered the building.

"Sweep kick, overhead slash, parry," Wade calls out each action as its performed. "I don't even need photographic memory to see that's your go to," he jabs. In a fit of rage, Kam stomps the floor, causing a chain of spikes to surge forward. In the spur of the moment, Wade pulls off a side flip as he violently slashes the spikes with his twin swords. Kam follows up his combination by drawing an axe from the ripple in the ground and tossing it forward with incredible power. Once again his attack his dodged.

"That's new," Wade whispers to himself as he dashes ahead in order to close the distance. Just before he gets within striking range, two more axes are thrown. Now sliding on his knees in a limbo fashion, the blades slightly shave off a thin layer of beard as he slips under with a near miss.

"Diagonal rising cut, forward thrust, roundhouse kick, Kam Fu?" Wade once again predicts each move accurately while jumping back on the defensive. However, the last stance taken throws him slightly off of his game. Now on all fours, positioned like a feral tiger, Kam swiftly pounces from wall to wall in every direction. He carefully searches for an opening while moving sporadically. With his sword now in his mouth, he spins in the air, flying towards Wade like a torpedo.

"I see, a corkscr– ah!" He's interrupted as he barely has time to react. Their swords collide for a brief moment with a metallic screech. Suddenly Kam ducks, and as his sword drops from his mouth, another ascends from the ground with a slight "shnnng" sound. He catches the falling sword and strikes upward, just barely stopping before it hits Wade's neck. The second sword is now pressed against his back as the two freeze in the moment. The view of this scene is truly picturesque. Wade gulps as he drops his two swords. Kam follows the notion and watches with an impartial look as the swords and spikes slowly sink into the ground. *Today's victory was nothing to brag about,* he thought. *It's only the first of many to come.* The boys gather themselves and face each other with a bow. Kameron wins.

"Again!" one of the boys shout out. Round two begins. A mysterious man hurriedly approaches. He's around 6'2", wearing a luxurious pea coat over a blazer with dark shades and a light stubble. If there was anything separating his appearance from that of a shady broker, it would be that he has a large silverback tattoo engraved on his neck.

"Oh, that must be my three o'clock!" Murphy shouts out in an overzealous tone.

"It must be," says the man as he takes off his glove and extends a hand. "I'm Arthur Prime, it's a pleasure, sir," he continues as he and Murphy shake hands.

"Oh no, of course, the pleasure is mine, Mr. Prime. I've been a fan since that stunt you pulled in the swamplands. To think you could really take down that many…ah, forget it. I'm getting ahead of myself. I'll be right back with your package, sir," Murphy says as he rushes to the back. At this point, every customer in the shop is inching their way toward the counter with their phones, peeking up in a horrible attempt to take off-guard photos.

"Here you are, sir, one copy of Phantom's Kiss 2: Deluxe Edition. This is actually the second one of these records sold today if you can believe it," Murphy announces as he glances at Jace with a side eye. Mr. Prime doesn't bother to follow his gaze as he adjusts his glasses and grabs the package. Taking advantage of the awkward silence, Jace suddenly chimes in.

"Hey, I know you! I'd recognize you from anywhere!" he says with his eyes narrowed. He loudly slams his hand on top of the counter as he makes his presence known.

"What are you saying? Of course you know him, he's the–"

"You're another man of culture! Trust me, I know one when I see one. Only the true fans know the deluxe edition is only available for in-store pickup!" Jace exclaims in admiration. He's too excited to even notice the gang of angry fans glaring away at his insolence.

"Relax, man, that's bad for business," Murphy grumbles with his face now bright red.   "Well I'll be going now. Thanks again, sir. I'll make sure Ms. Booth leaves a five-star review," says Mr. Prime as he completely ignores Jace's erratic outburst. Just as he's walking away, the swarm of fans bum rush him before he gets to the door. In the midst of the chaos, a chubby fan in glasses grabs his shoulder but is instantly flipped on his back, knocking down several racks of CDs on his way down. The sight of this immediately sends Jace in a rage. He quickly takes a step forward, sending a shadow forth but draws it back at the last second. After exchanging glances with a now livid Jace, Mr. Prime crouches down as his bones twist and break, morphing into some sort of hybrid creature. A long set of fangs protrude from his mouth as patches of hair grow around his face and from his knuckles. His nose is now slightly elongated with shades of red and blue surfacing. There's barely any trace left of the imposing man from before. In its place stands a ferocious beast of a simian nature.

"Ah!"

"Oh my gosh! It's his Mandrill form!"

`"I can't believe I'm seeing this up close, what's going on?!"

"It's the beast of the swamplands!" Every single fan, including an astonished Murphy, watches in awe seeing Arthur Prime in action. He suddenly lunges towards the exit, completely hurdling over the pile of bewildered fans. The impact of the jump leaves a small crater on the linoleum floors. The one on the receiving end of the attack is a hooded thief who used the sudden presence of a celebrity to sneak merchandise outside unnoticed. He crashes into the unsuspecting thief, rendering him unconscious with a powerful kick.

"Tony, no!" A cry can be heard from a chubby man in glasses. It turns out the man who grabbed him earlier was just a decoy. The fans go crazy with roaring applause as they're completely astonished at seeing his primate form in person. Another cry is let out, but this time it's Arthur Prime's triumphant battle roar. As the cheers and jeers continue, Jace hastily picks up all of the merchandise that was knocked down. After reverting back to his human form, Mr. Prime returns to apologize for the damage, noting that he'll pay for it later. As he walks away, he once again exchanges glances with a glaring Jace. For a split second, there was the type of dangerous spark in their eyes that seemed like it could turn into a raging fire at any moment. Prime's eyes narrow as he starts to put something together, but he quickly changes his mind as if it's not important enough to think over.

"Che!" Jace grits his teeth as he watches the arrogant hero exit the shop.

"Hmph, must've been my imagination," Mr. Prime sneers as he throws his tattered coat over his shoulder. There's no amount of crime too small for Arthur Prime.

"You ready to throw in the towel yet?" asks an exhausted Kam in between breaths.

"I should be asking you that. I skipped PT this morning just for this," Wade replies with a slight grin. Gathering the last of his strength, Kam throws a series of jabs followed by an overhand right. Wade carefully blocks each jab, and just before the right connects, he steps to the side. He then pushes Kam's elbow inwards and counters with a straight knee.

"Gah!" Kam spits out as he falls to the ground writhing in pain. With this another match concludes; Wade wins. "That was a good hit, you bastard," Kam says as he gathers himself up. "To be honest that was all the strength I had left, I'm beat," Wade replies.

"Yeah, let's call it here. Lunch is probably ready by now anyways," Kam adds as the two bow in unison. Just before they get to the door, it's violently swung open.

"Guess what happened today?! Some rat bastard named Arthur Prime trashed Murphy's shop!" Jace shouts out, flailing his arms in an exaggerated manner.

"The bodyguard hero?!" The two boys look at each other in disbelief.

"Wasn't he supposed to be working for Mayor Hamilton?" Kam asks.

"No, you're thinking of Senator Booth. Prime was assigned as his bodyguard while he's in Sapphire City backing Mayor Hamilton on his campaign for governor. Personally he's got my vote," Wade confirms.

"Well either way, he's no hero to me," Jace retorts. As he says this, you can see layers of darkness slowly seep through each corner of the room. "Oh, wait, sorry I forgot to tap the sign," Jace suddenly remembers, now backpedaling towards the door. Rays of sunshine make their way back in with each step. Just outside of the dojo, there's a large yellow sign. Even though it's pretty worn down, you can still make out the word "Discipline" in bold black letters. Jace taps the sign twice and bangs his chest to top it off.

"So what did y'all do today?" he asks as he returns from the ritual.

"Apparently I learned Kam Fu," Wade says jokingly.

"Damn, I was hoping that didn't stick…" The boys all share a laugh as they head for lunch. Another eventful day for the Hero Trinity.

****

Four years ago in Morocco…

A beautiful Asian woman in a jet black catsuit creeps into an abandoned warehouse. Besides a few empty crates and dusty machines, nothing or no one else seems to occupy this vast space. She ties up her long black hair with a sharp pin resembling a dagger while examining every corner of the shabby building intently. Her eyes dart back and forth repeatedly as if expecting to be taken at any moment. The echo from her heels deafen with each step, the sound getting lost in the tension in the air. She stops abruptly as she locks eyes with a single entity.

"So you're him. The man who survived…" she calls out. A hooded man is sitting on a makeshift throne with two fingers pressed against his temple. There's a glimmer in his eye as if he's remembering something horrific. Still in a trance, he fixes his mouth to speak.

"I am a man that stood upon the precipice of death yet could not leap," he murmurs, looking downward.

"Well that's a hell of a way of saying zombie," the woman nonchalantly retorts. "Zombie? No. If you want a zombie, I believe this would be more to your liking," he immediately replies. With a wave of his hand, the ground beneath their feet begins to quake. Several pairs of arms simultaneously sprout from the ground, but what rears its ugly head is a figure that's not quite all the way there. Small pieces of flesh hang from the legs, torso, and face of each creature as they rise to the surface. They all turn and face the woman, standing at attention.

"Okay I set myself up for that one…" she mumbles to herself. The conversation then goes as follows:

"Look, I need your help."

"How did you even find me, child?"

"Child?"

"…."

"Chasing ghosts is never easy, but I have my sources. Though I didn't expect I'd have to come all the way to Morocco."

"Well, for this, I commend you, but why should I help the likes of you?"

"Do I really look that dangerous?"

"…."

"It's because you weren't always a John Doe. I know who you are, I know what they did to you. You're more than a toe tag."

She slips him a singed ID card while backpedaling with her hands raised, showing a display of innocence. Snapping back to reality, John slowly fixes his gaze upon the mysterious woman who has brought upon him the sole remnants of his true identity.

"And I know what it's like to give everything for something you thought was bigger than yourself. Bigger than all of us. They took too much for a worthless cause, now it's time to get it back in blood," she declares.

John shakes his head in shame and with few words replies, "A worthless cause indeed…" As he says this, he unveils himself, exposing semi-decayed flesh. Judging from the absence of color in his face and small cracks along his jaw, this is a man that has been reanimated. Almost every word he speaks is in a somber tone. It's as if he dreads his existence more and more as each day passes. However, everything changed the moment that one card returned to his hands. What returned with it was a sliver of light in his eyes that one had thought to have been long lost. A shred of humanity had been restored. John rises from the throne and makes his way to the exit with a spring in his step. As he walks off, he lightly tosses the card at one of his nightmarish minions. The corpse slowly descends into the ground, holding it gently as it bows its head on the way down. John then goes on to explain the events that took place fourteen years ago while they make their leave. The rest of the minions sluggishly trail behind them. The disturbing sound of chattering teeth and rattling bones fill the already frosty night air.

"Oh, and by the way….call me Alias," the woman insists. Only chaos and destruction follow this pernicious alliance.

Chapter 3: Asylum

Twelve years ago....

A father tenderly holds his son on his lap as he reads him a story. His curly hair is swaying back and forth while imitating the mighty roar of a dragon.

"I am Balthazar, hear me rawr!" he bellows.

"Ah!" High-pitched screams come from a chubby little boy in plaid pajamas. He suddenly bolts across the room, accidentally knocking his father's glasses to the side. With long naturally curly hair and a husky build, Andre and Jason Collins are two sides of the same coin. The only time he doesn't look like a spitting image of his father is when he's somewhere tucked away cowering in fear at the littlest thing. This boy was certainly a far cry from the burly six-foot-one and well-toned Jace who is usually seen parading around wearing a foolish grin, one-third of the Hero Trinity.

"Really, Dre? You tryna push him away so he won't be clinging to you the whole field trip, huh?" a voice calls out. In the doorway stands a lovely caramel-skinned woman in a lab coat, delicately stroking her long amber hair. She sends a playful wink towards the young Jace. Her sly grin combined with her discerning eyes bewitch you to the point where it's blatantly obvious you're in the presence of an imposing woman. Chanelle Collins was undoubtedly a treasure.

"Listen, you boys better not take all day, okay? Stay on schedule. I'll be going ahead to get the machines up and running before the presentation starts. Love you babies," she says, blowing a loving kiss just before making her exit.

"Alright, Jace, let's get ready for Mom's big day!" Andre happily shouts as he springs up and collects his glasses. Just a few blocks away dwelling on the edge of the city of Pearl's Gate, there's a young Kam sloppily tying a tie as he tries to emulate the actions of his stern father, Julius Scott.

"Ha-ha, well I appreciate the effort, but you didn't have to take my words so seriously, kiddo," he chuckles.

"To be a man, you have to see a man," Kam recites with his head held high.

"That's right, but a man isn't something you can copy and paste. Every step you take reveals a different path to becoming the person you're meant to be. I'm sure you'll grow into a fine man one day, Kameron. Keep your head held high just as you are," he states with a proud look.

"Yes, sir!" Kam replies joyously. "Hey, Dad, can we go get some pancakes before the trip?" he suddenly asks.

"That's fine, but let's hurry, you don't want to miss your pop's big speech, do you?" he replies with a smirk.

"No way! I'll go get my shoes!" Kam immediately responds. Just before they reach the door, they stop at a particular mantle and spend a brief moment staring in silence.

"Don't forget to give your mom a kiss, bud," Mr. Scott whispers. Following his father's words, little Kam grabs a small picture frame and holds it to him close. A quiet "mwah" can be heard as he gives it a gentle kiss. It gets a little easier to say goodbye each time.

"Sapphire City: the cornerstone of peace and prosperity. A city thriving with life as students and entrepreneurs from all over the world gather to contribute to the rise of a new technological empire. Backed by one of the largest enterprises of the twenty-first century, CORE labs, it quickly became the staple of pharmaceutical advancement and modern genetics. I am standing here in the center of the city right outside of the famous Pembrooke Hotel, the location for the grand reveal of CORE labs latest miracle. The release of the new air purifier/bacterial neutralizer is expected to be the current frontrunner in the race for materials designed to prevent the next global pandemic. Students from our very own Patriot's Heart Elementary have been specially selected to witness and participate in this monumental achievement. Furthermore the two chief engineers who headlined this project have come to present it live and in person. It's truly a blessing to be in the presence of greatness here today. I'm Laura Watson, and this is your channel two news." A reporter can be heard describing the events of the day as Mr. Scott and young Kam frantically rush into the hotel building. While hastily making his way through the lobby, he catches the attention of Andre Collins. The two exchange nods, seemingly reading each other's minds as he nudges Kam towards his way.

"Kam!" Jace shouts as he runs full speed with open arms.

"Alright, kids, let's find our seats; it's about to begin," a teacher sharply commands. "Welp, that's my cue, go and find your friends, boys," Mr. Collins says as he heads over to join the other chaperones. In the far corner of the hotel is a luxurious conference room. Lovely eighteenth century Western European wallpaper grace the walls, and the floor is decorated with intricate golden floral patterns. The first thing you notice upon arrival is a large crystal chandelier winding down in a double spiral shape. Next is a huge stage with dozens of chairs facing forward in its direction. In the corner of the room, there's a buffet table packed with various finger foods and coupe glasses. Hanging directly over the podium is a large blue banner which reads: Creators Overseeing Revolutionary Experimentation. Below the banner are three small cylindrical machines, all covered with a black tarp. Heading the front row is about twenty students from Patriot's Heart Elementary, Mrs. Pope's third grade class. The rest of the space is occupied by scientists, engineers, young scholars, and journalists as they lie in wait to witness the glorious events of the day. Various chatter can be heard throughout the room, including the playful banter of a certain group of students. Some lighthearted teasing can be heard from children: Cheyenne Fredricks, her twin brother Elliot, Princeton Campbell, and none other than Jason Collins, who noticed two of their classmates holding hands.

"Oh, Kam and Ashley sitting in a tree, K-I-S-S-I-N-G!" they all chant in unison.

"Shut up! My dad's right over there!" Kam shouts while blushing. Looking around the room, Jace notices a certain seat in particular is empty.

"Hey, where'd *my* dad go?!" he says as his head bobbles around in every direction. All the way in the back of the room, an unpleasant conversation can be heard from a married couple. "After this you'll have more time at home, right?" the man asks.

"I didn't want to tell you this until later, but they wants us to start working on the new model as soon as possible," the woman replies.

"What? This was supposed to be our time! You can't keep running at their beck and call!" the man cries out. Peering eyes start to wander in their direction.

"Look, Dre, when it comes to changing the world, I'm glad to play this much of a role. You know I do this for something bigger than myself," the woman states.

"Che (Shay), you and Jason ARE my world. I can care less about anything else! Why does it have to be you? People can save themselves!" he says with his arms spread out.

"Can we not do this right now? Please, just not today, Dre. We'll talk later," the woman desperately pleads.

"I'm getting real sick of hearing that…" Mr. Collins hangs his head down as the fight with his dear wife ends in defeat. With this the two part ways and the presentation begins. "November 10th, 2008, remember this day, ladies and gentlemen. It is the day we proudly tread the waters of evolution," Dr. Collins begins.

"That's right, people, we, Chief Engineers Julius Scott and Chanelle Collins, present to you CORE Laboratories newest invention: The Particle Packer," Dr. Scott follows up while uncovering the tarp. The two continue playing off of each other as they further explain.

"Since long ago, people like us have been striving to protect the world from biological warfare, the lethal T36 being no exception. Ever since we all discovered that the virus mainly targeted children, especially those that were non-vaccinated, CORE Labs has been finding ways to guarantee them a safer environment. Our efforts have yielded many results, but with this new machine, you can rest assured our loved ones shall fear no more. I promise you a pandemic that devastating will never be seen again. As you can see, the mechanics are fairly simple. On the outside, it's no different than your standard purification system."

"However, we've discovered a new compound, which we named Bacithium Nitrite. Its basic chemical makeup completely annihilates any harmful bacteria in the surrounding area."   "To top it off, this machine is equipped with a state-of-the-art ion generator with the capability to completely eradicate virtually any virus on an atomic level, including the T36 virus that plagued this very nation five years ago."

"That's right, Dr. Scott, but because the Particle Packer has quite the substantial energy output, there was a slight delay on its approval. The fact that we can present this current model to you today is truly a milestone in modern engineering and pharmaceutical science, and we hope to see these at each major manufacturer by the time….." The doctors' words grow more and more distant as Mr. Collins heads for the door with a pack of cigarettes in hand. He takes a quick glance at his wife and his now elated son before he makes his exit.

"Hey, hey, Kam, have you seen my dad anywhere?" young Jace asks as he notices a particular seat is once again vacant.

"Maybe he went outside?" young Kam answers with his shoulders shrugged.

"That's exactly where he went. I just seen him leave a minute ago." This reply comes from little Ashley Harris, who untangles her hands from Kam's grasp to point towards the door. "Then I'm going, too!" Jace shouts.

"Hey, wait for us! Let's go, guys," Kam calls out. Elliot and Princeton join the two boys as they stealthily make their escape. It doesn't take long for one of the boys to notice there's a few members of the gang missing.

"Sorry, guys, I'm gonna stay behind. My sister's coming to get me soon, and I want to enjoy as much as I can," Ashley whispers.

"If she's staying, then I am, too," Cheyenne decides.

Before they sneak off, Ashley grabs Kam and whispers, "Just be careful out there. If Mrs. Pope finds out you guys left, I'll tell her Princeton got sick and you had to rush him to the bathroom. I'll say the others followed you out of concern."

"Thanks for making me the hero of the story. Make sure you tell her it was a job only I can handle," Kam jokes.

"Hurry up and go, silly. Believe it or not, they really do need you, Kam," Ashley says with a kind smile. The simultaneous "ohhhs and ahhhs" coming from the crowd make for the perfect opportunity for the kids to slip away unnoticed. Just outside of the grand hotel is your typical city scene. Pedestrians flooding the streets with a small cup of coffee on hand, vendors serving their famous cheesesteaks and franks, and groups of homeless men and women setting up camp in front of a few popular shops. Crossing guards can be seen directing the surging flow of traffic while the boys-in-blue keep the chaotic crowds to a minimum as a means to protect some of the greatest minds of the twenty-first century gathered inside. Posted in a nearby alley with his foot against the wall, inhaling a large puff from a cigarette, is the frustrated Andre Collins.

"Dad! Dad! You're missing Mom's big speech!" Jace exclaims in a frenzy.

"Whoa, calm down, Jace, what are you doing here?" he replies. "Why did you drag your friends all the way out here? I'm not responsible for anybody else's kids you know," he complains. He takes another hit of his cigarette before flicking it away. "Look, I'm sorry, buddy. How are you enjoying the trip? Your mom sure is something else, isn't she?" He says with a wry smile. "Anyways, these two must be the Elliot and Princeton I heard so much about at home, huh? Nice to meet you. I'm Jason's father." Mr. Collins nods as he makes his introduction.

"Wait, two? Where's Kam?" Jace asks with a puzzled look. Peeking his little head inside of a car window is a grinning Kam making conversation with the driver.

"What you doing out here, kid? It's cold out, why don't you hop inside and warm up for a bit?" the driver insists.

"No, it's okay, my friends are waiting for me over there," Kam replies.

"Oh I see. So tell me, Kammie, why isn't my little sister with you? You two are usually joined at the hip," the driver asks with a raised brow. Kam drops his head in embarrassment upon hearing this. The mystery driver just so happens to be a sassy teenage girl with natural locks flowing down to her shoulders and vibrant hazel eyes. Around her neck is an Egyptian style necklace with an elegant blue pendant in the center. Decorating her wrists are four charm bracelets, two on each arm, with all of them full of various animals and other lucky charms. This girl was Hazel Harris, elder sister of Ashley Harris.

"Mhm," she says with her eyes narrowed. "Well look, Kammie, I'm gonna need for you to head back inside before you get in trouble, okay?" she demands.

"Okay, see you later, big sis!" he happily shouts as he crosses the street.

"Don't forget to look both ways! NO, KAM, WAIT!" she desperately yells out. SCRRRRRRRRRRT! BOOM! The ear-splitting screeching of brakes fill the air, followed by a resounding explosion. BOOM! BOOM! BOOM! BOOM! The thundering eruptions continue causing a chain reaction. Combined with the deafening sound of clashing metal and collapsing bricks, this phenomenon felt big enough to shift the earth off of its axis. The concussive force alone sent Kam flying backwards like a frisbee.

"Mom!" Jace's blood-curdling scream echoes as he realizes the painful truth behind this horrid occurrence. The imploding building before him was none other than the Pembrooke Hotel. The place where the scientific achievement of the century was to be broadcasted for the world to see is now a searing calamity, with a lone white truck responsible for the wreckage. "Affordable Lawn and Landscaping" can just barely be made out from the side of the demolished fertilizer truck. The sound of hundreds of men, women, and children screaming for their lives are heard throughout this large corner of the city. The rancid smell of burning flesh contaminates the air with each breath.

"Dad? Dad?! Dad!" Jace repeatedly cries out as he frantically tugs on his father's coat. His father's expressionless face only deepens Jace's feeling of complete helplessness.

Andre Collins point of view:

I hear my son calling my name, but I just can't bring myself to look in his direction. The only thing I can do is hold him tight as I witness the massacre before my eyes. I hold him tighter and tighter, just like when I read him a story. No, even tighter. Papa's here, son, papa's here. Wait, what is that little girl doing? Is she really trying to run full speed into the building? There's not even a single sign of a way in what's she trying to do? What's she yelling; I can barely hear her. Ah, something about her little sister, she must have been inside. Should I follow her brave and instinctual reaction? Should I be clawing and scratching my way in despite the dozens of policemen barricading the front entrance? There's debris falling every second and flames almost completely engulfing the surrounding area. What kind of help would I even be? No, that's wrong. I have to see her again. I don't want our last moment together to be an argument, anything but that. Does she even know? Does she know how much I love her? Wait a minute, I feel like a shred of warmth left my body. Jace? What are you doing? Whose body are you trying so desperately to drag over here? I didn't even notice you left my side until now, yet here you are, saving someone's life. Even at this age you've already surpassed me.

Though he's covered in soot, I can tell by his low-cut hair and that expensive coat that it's Julius' boy. Wait, what's going on?! These boys are...my boys are in pain! They just dropped down out of nowhere, writhing in agony. They're screeching their lungs out, reaching out to me screaming my name. Spikes?! Why are there spikes coming out of this boy's body? Through his eyes!? What do I do to stop this?! How is he still alive with this many spears coming out of his chest? Wait, Jace? Jason?! JASON! My son....the devil has my son! The devil's taking away my son! All these hands, they're trying so hard to drag him down, groaning as if they're longing for him! Who's doing this to me?! Huh? Who damned my son?! Is my wife still burning?! Will she continue to burn in the next life? Nah, nah, nah, nah, I refuse to let it go down like this. I WILL save my son.

"Hey! Hey! What are you doing!? Get away from my son!" Mr. Collins exclaims as he rushes to the rescue. Just before he's within his grasp, Jace is completely submerged into the earth as dozens of demonic shadows pull him into the depths below.

"Chanelle! Jason's gone! His friend is dying! Look at him, Che, he's impaled! CHANELLE!" he wails in a state of delirium. He looks absolutely mortified as the truth finally sinks in. His voice will never be able to reach his wife again.

"He-he…ha-ha-ha-ha-ha," he lets out a soft chuckle before being escorted away by the paramedics. He couldn't take a look back, even if he tried, for he can only look forward, paralyzed by utter shock. There's not even a tiny sliver of light left in his eyes nor a shred of hope in his heart. The slow descent into madness bathed in a sinister shroud of darkness.

****

Two weeks ago..

"For four whole years we've prepared, in your case even longer, but now…now we strike. Just remember, Alias, that this is bigger than your petty need for revenge. I'm also willing to sacrifice thousands of lives to catch the bigger fish, but the fact still remains that we signed over our consent for those trials. Don't mistake my leniency for conformity. The mission's success is imperative above all else," John Doe asserts as he watches Alias sharpen her knives.   " W e l l that much is obvious seeing as that I need you just as much as you need me. Besides, I wanna see their world burn just as much as you," Alias replies with a wink. She blows the specks of trimmings off of her blades as she continues. "Though it's funny you mention fish. The funniest thing of all are those who swim too close to the surface…just begging to be gutted alive. Far be it for me to deny them their penance," she states, violently stabbing the table with the freshly sharpened knife.

"It certainly is well within our rights. The irony behind it all is that the last thing they will ever see is themselves, their last breath whisked away by their own hands," John agrees. He slowly nods before he turns around and walks away with his arms folded behind his back. Alias grabs the knife from the table and heads in the opposite direction. The increasing sound of rattling chains fill the sinister air.

"MMMM! MMMM!" a voice desperately cries out through a mouthful of duct tape. In the far end of the room is a docker frantically flailing his arms and legs as he sees a man approaching. He screams in sheer terror while watching as his entrails decorate the entire floor. Holding the knife is a bearded man in a skull cap and overalls viciously pulling the docker's organs apart. The docker recognizes this man instantly, and before his eyes roll to the back of his head, a stream of tears can be seen flowing from the corner of them. He spends his final moments peering through the looking glass, for the face of the man who had taken his life from him was none other than his own. The man loudly chuckles as he slicks his hair back, tying it down with a small pin in the shape of a dagger.

"Gotta love a man that's poetic," Alias says as she wipes the blood from her knife on his overalls. There's a storm coming for Sapphire City.

Chapter 4: Deception

Present day..

"Sapphire City, the cornerstone of peace and prosperity," Alias recites as she takes in a deep breath of the nostalgic home air.

"Is that what they tell you to say?" John asks with a hint of sarcasm.

"That's just one of the many lies they spoon feed the youth," she answers, showing a solemn expression.

"Shall we go over the plan one last time now that we've arrived?" John asks.

"I believe that's unnecessary, but if it's for you, then it's as you wish. Though after becoming so many people in a day, I'm worried you might not recognize this pretty little face anymore," Alias jokingly pouts.

"Very funny, my dear, but let's not lose focus on what's important. Infiltrating Holland Central Bank is no small feat, let alone impersonating William Holland himself. Don't get cocky just because we so happened to have stumbled upon his master password from a data leak in the black market. Remember to speak as little as possible. Mannerisms and key phrases are enough. You know whose name to search for, but there's files other than his that can be extracted," John asserts.

"I don't know how to tell you this but…this ain't my first rodeo, chief," Alias retorts after letting out a sigh. "Let me guess, next you're gonna remind me to rendezvous at the abandoned church in Pearl's Gate," she mocks.

"What I was going to say was that I'll have not one but two of my top brass standing guard in the vicinity. Something tells me to be extra cautious in this city," John replies.

"Well your hunch is right. All they've been talking about on the news lately is how Arthur Prime has been parading around here playing hero. If there's any type of wrench thrown in our plans, it would be that. It's best we steer clear of him for now," Alias advises. "Understood. Are there any other notable presences in the area worth mentioning?" John asks with his hand gripping his chin.

"Not that I know of, but there's one man you should always watch out for…Let's just say people call him the boogeyman," Alias answers with an icy stare. Her eyes seem to see something far within her reach, yet close enough to return her gaze. Through those eyes, John can sense the eminent presence of danger. *It seems everybody's afraid of something,* he thinks to himself.

"Do people really still go to the mall to pick up chicks?" a skeptical-looking Wade asks while scratching at his brow.

"Hey, four handsome rich guys out shopping, I mean come on! They'll practically fall into our laps!" Jace replies reassuringly on their stroll along the city.

"Handsome?" a sour-faced Kam retorts as he dodges an incoming slap on the back. "Y'all can do whatever y'all want, I actually came to shop. It's getting cold outside, so it's about time I throw on something nice," he states. He then secretly nudges Jace, and with his hand covering his mouth, he mutters, "But if you run into any fine little joints along the way, just know I got your back, bro."

"Welp that's one down to party, what about you, Joe?" Jace asks with bulging eyes.

"It wouldn't hurt to try, I mean there's a first time for everything, right?" This candid reply comes from a lanky boy wearing a cashmere and silk parka over a velvet school blazer. He's almost as tall as the six-foot-four Kam but has a slightly slimmer build and wavy slicked back hair. This boy is Joseph Holland, beloved brother of the hero trinity.

"Don't be like them, Joe; you can get any woman you want just by being you," Wade chimes in. "But you guys are on your own with this one. I have to stop by the bank and tie up some loose ends. Don't do anything I wouldn't do, okay?" he says with a wink. He breaks off and heads towards the end of the strip. A black Rolls Royce pulls up to the entrance of Holland Central. Escorted out of the vehicle is none other than the illustrious William Holland. Treading carefully in his custom-made Oxfords and three-piece suit, he's accompanied by two large bodyguards both dressed in a trench coat, scarf, fedora, and shades.

"Well you guys don't look suspicious at all. Remember, gentlemen, no speaking roles," Alias chuckles to herself as she signals for the undead to wait at the door. The loud clacking of incoming footsteps barely seem to faze the young receptionist at the counter glued to her phone. "Yes, how may I assist you today?" She greets Mr. Holland without breaking her gaze. "Ah, so you did notice someone standing here," he replies sarcastically. She looks up with a bitter face, but that doesn't last long. Her eyes nearly pop out of her skull as she glances back and forth between two images. Both are of the same imposing older man, but only one is directly meeting her gaze with a suitcase in hand wearing a gentle smile.

"Like, oh my God! I am so sorry, Mr. Holland! I swear I'm usually never on my phone, but it's been slow all day I just–" she says while nearly prostrating herself but is interrupted midway.

"It's fine, Claire, just don't make it a habit, okay?" Mr. Holland replies. He heads toward the elevator, giving a small wave to several employees on the way.

"He knows my name!" Claire joyously exclaims.

"Um, probably because of your name tag, Claire," a fellow receptionist leans in and reminds her. Both the highest and lowest floors of the colossal facility are widely known for its top-flight security. Only one man has the right to walk straight into the largest office of the entire building, bypassing each and every guard without so much as a look. This man just so happens to currently be inside said office with all of the curtains drawn.

"Just a walk in the park," Alias mumbles to herself as she taps away at the keyboard. She then sticks a flash drive into the computer and patiently waits for the bank files to upload. An uncharacteristically menacing smile forms on the face of the gallant Mr. Holland...double.

"It feels like the world is ours already, right, John?" he boasts with his fingers pressed together in a villainous pose. Radio silence on the other end.

"We hope to see you again soon, Mr. Holland!" Claire loudly shouts, practically oozing with desperation.

"Mr Holl–, Dad?!" A voice calls out while walking through the double doors.

"Ah, the prodigal son has returned," he says while extending his arms for a hug.

"Funny I should be saying that to you. I would return the love, Dad, but... ya know..." Wade points at the large suitcase and small binder both in their grasp respectively. "Well I should be on my way. I have some business to handle, but we can catch up at home, right?" Wade asks, cutting the reunion short.

"Sounds like a plan. I'll see you and Joseph at home then. Remind the misses how much I love her, will ya?" Mr. Holland replies with a small nod before heading to the exit. A slightly puzzled look befalls Wade's face, but he quickly gathers himself and trots ahead.

"That was a little too close for comfort if you ask me. Alright, boys, cover me, it's time to let my hair down," Alias commands the two minions who've been patiently waiting outside. This time she decides to take the form of a ravishing fair-skinned woman with curly blonde hair. Her voluptuous body is draped in a $40,000 mink coat and six-inch pumps. She applies some red lipstick while thinking to herself, "Hmph, baby girl almost looks as good as me. Maybe getting more in touch with my feminine side might be a good idea after all." Making a clean get away, she fiercely struts along the strip, looking like something straight out of a magazine. "Yo….Yo who is that?!" a man exclaims, catching a glimpse at the stunning woman prancing down the opposite end of the sidewalk.

"We already struck out at the mall, let's not push our luck, dude," a somber reply comes from a noticeably fatigued Joe. Kam immediately fires back.

"Nah, YOU struck out at the mall. I didn't even–"

"Nah, bro, who is THAT?!" Jace loudly interjects before foolishly attempting to cross the street, despite the rush hour traffic. His unwavering gaze is fixed upon a gorgeous woman with long beautiful brown locks flowing down her back. She's only wearing sweatpants and a plain crop top under her coat, but the simplicity of her wardrobe ironically brings all types of unwanted attention towards her heavenly face. The most enticing thing of all is her dazzling hazel eyes. Kam quickly throws his hand in front Jace, bringing him to a halt.

"Let me show you boys how it's done," he says while adjusting his watch. The boys cross the street with Kam leading the way, but just before he's about to make his introduction, the woman turns around with a furrowed brow. Seeing her face up close causes Kam to immediately stumble back.

His heart practically bursts through his chest, and as he scrambles to catch his breath, he mutters out the name "Ashley?!"

"Excuse me?!" she answers with an agitated expression. He instantly snaps back into reality and apologizes.

"Sorry, you just reminded me of my long-lost friend for a second. Let me start over and at least introduce myself."

"Mhmmm…so what, you don't recognize me anymore, Kammie?" she replies with a now disappointed look.

"Yo, what?! Hazel, is that you?!" Kam is absolutely shocked upon seeing such a familiar face. "You look more stunning than ever," he adds.

"I see you've grown into a handsome man yourself I mean you're so tall! What are you, like seven-foot?!" Hazel responds back.

"You're in the ballpark," he replies with a shrug. "I'm about 6'4", 185 pounds. You tryna scout me?" he chuckles.

"Boy, shut up!" she shouts playfully. "But all jokes aside, you've grown into a fine young man. I can sense something different in you, but it's hard to explain…" she says with her eyes narrowed.

"Pardon me, I figured I'd make my introduction as well. I'm Joseph Holland, it's a pleasure," Joe chimes in.

"Well look at you being all polite! What a respectful young man," Hazel replies with a smile. Her face quickly changes to an irritated expression as she notices a large pair of eyes fixed on her. "Uh, is that the chubby boy who used to stare at me with those hungry little bug eyes?" she asks with her finger pointed towards Jace.

"Sadly yes," Kam answers with a sigh.

"Nah, nah, that was probably somebody else, girl. It's nice to meet you though. I'm Jason," he announces.

"Girl? You better call me by my name," Hazel snaps back.

"Oh, sorry, uh…" He looks down at her necklace for a brief second, then back into her eyes. "Queen Priestess," he continues. "Anyways it was nice to see you again, Kammie, this was definitely the highlight of my day. I gotta hurry up and drop these bags off, but I hope we can continue this conversation another time," she says.

Kam leans in for a hug and replies, "Most definitely. How can I get in contact with you again though?"

"Don't worry, now that I know you're here, I won't be too hard to reach," Hazel assures. "Well that's a vague answer. By the way why do they call you Queen?" Jace interrupts. "Because there's a whole new world out there beyond your understanding." As she says this, he just barely catches a glimpse of a green aura dancing around her entire body. Something like elephant tusks protrude from her jaw, and there was a certain gravity in her presence that almost dared you to look away. With those words, the boys decide to part ways, leaving the mystery to imagination. They continue to wander around the city for a couple of hours. Just as they got tired of walking, they realized they had been subconsciously heading straight toward the bank.

"We might as well sit on the bench and wait for Wade since we're here," Joe insists with his shoulders shrugged.

"I guess there's no other options," Kam decides.

"Well it certainly wasn't hard to find you guys!" a voice yells out. A wild-eyed girl with light blonde pigtail buns is suddenly standing right in front of the three boys. She has her hands resting behind her back and a chipper expression can be seen on her face like there's nowhere else she'd rather be than here.

"So show of hands, who all did their homework today?" she asks with her hands raised, revealing two strange objects that she had been previously hiding. On each hand are brass knuckles with spikes coming from each finger slot and wing-shaped blades sticking out of each end of the weapon. This was a weapon designed with the intent to kill but also meant for the victim to feel each and every slice. This was how animals toyed with their prey.

"Go find your brother, then head home, Joe," Jace demands with a stern look. Suddenly the city seems to be a long way from peace and prosperity.

Chapter 5: Fight of the Century

A visibly distraught Joe rushes into the bank at full speed.

"Whoa, looks like you beat me to the punch. This wouldn't be as fun if the whole gang's not here," the pigtailed girl blurts out as he zips by. Kam and Jace turn to each other in utter confusion. The first to say what each other had been thinking is Jace.

"Yo, you know this girl?"

"Nah, that goth cheerleader cosplay is definitely more of a you thing," Kam emphasizes. She looks down at her black mini skirt, then looks back up with a glum expression. It seems like she's starting to say something, but she suddenly lunges in to attack. Right before she lands the first blow, she stops and starts to applaud at the now fully suited up duo.

"Yay! It's about time you two took this seriously!" she shouts in excitement. "Ready? Okay!" she cheers out before performing a series of flips. In the middle of a back handspring, a sharp blade pops out from her shoe. The boys both step in the opposite direction, dodging the incoming flip kick.

"Smart move getting us masked up in public by the way, bro. I didn't even notice until she said something," Jace calls out, adjusting his mask.

"I know, now focus. This girl is definitely one basket short of a picnic," Kam whispers. By the time she lands, two daggers are flying at her jugular with remarkable precision. She dodges by hitting a perfect split. With her hands planted on the ground, she lifts herself up, twirling around in a handstand before setting back on her feet.

"Oh, that was a close one," she giggles while staring at the park bench ahead. It had been forcefully uprooted from the ground due to the impact of the flying daggers. "By the way, I wouldn't let these boot blades hit you if I were you. Just one touch can paralyze an elephant!" the pigtailed girl warns, still giggling.

"Okay, enough with the elephants today," Jace complains.

"You know what, bro, you haven't put in any real work lately; you handle this. I'll be on crowd control," Kam pokes fun at Jace while backing up.

"With pleasure," Jace answers with shimmering eyes. "Alright, lil' girl, you better get serious cuz I'm not holding back," Jace warns, cracking his knuckles.

"Well I would crack mine, but that doesn't seem too lady-like, now does it?" she replies with her finger pressed on her lip in thought. "Hope you're ready to get your ass handed to you!" the girl warns. "Okay, wow, I've always wanted to say that!" She blushes while doing small little jumps in the air.

"Whoa, you can at least tease me a little before going all the way," Jace fires back before charging in. The pigtailed girl starts to run toward Jace but is instantly tripped up and suspended in thin air. A shadow ghoul attempts to hold her in place, but a powerful swing from her bladed weapon causes it to dissipate before Jace's arrival. He flies in with a spinning whip kick, and she's propelled upward. On the way up, she groans and slices the air with a backhand, only just missing his leg. At the moment her blades zip passed his foot, they start to glow a sinister purple, and he's suddenly pulled up towards her body. She grabs his foot mid-air and tosses him forward before she hits the ground. They loudly slam into the pavement, both grimacing in pain from the impact. In the background is a confused Kam, completely baffled at the sight of this counterattack.

"Gr! Come on, Sasha, you're better than this!" the pigtailed girl says to herself, slapping both her cheeks.

"Who?" Jace asks.

"Oh, didn't I tell you? I'm Sasha Ivanov, otherwise known as the 'Mask Diva!'" she dramatically introduces herself with her hands on her hips.

"Huh? The famous internet sensation with over a million followers? Who cares!" Jace says, desperately trying to hide his excitement.

Somewhere in the distance you can hear a voice yell out, "We're The Hero Trinity, nice to meet you!"

"Welp that's one new sub, te-he-he," she chuckles. With her guard now down, Jace swoops in ready to attack. Sasha throws the first punch, but it's countered with an axe kick to the arm. She then follows with a left hook, but before it lands, her fist is grabbed by a large smoky hand. She follows up by leaning in for a head butt, but Jace quickly steps behind her and connects with a front kick. She stumbles a few yards forward before twisting around and falling on her back. Just as her back hits the ground, she springs back up with a kip-up, looking like something straight out of a Kung-Fu film. By the time Sasha tries to get back on the defensive, it's already too late. A powerful crescent kick to the stomach temporarily sends her body into shock. Her blades once again start to glow, emitting a sinister purple. She throws a sharp uppercut, but it's carefully dodged before it lands. As Jace snaps his head back, it's suddenly pulled back into her fist against his will. The small spikes extending from Sasha's knuckles slightly sink into his chin, causing him to cry out. At this point, Kam can be seen stepping forward with his eyes narrowed and fists clenched.

"Ha-ha-ha, just when I was feeling untouchable! Good hit, girl!" Jace compliments. He's suddenly forced to shuffle backwards in order to avoid the barrage of incoming kicks from her poison-coated boots. He uses a shadow ghoul to toss him several feet in the air before she closes the distance.

"Oh no you don't!" Sasha shouts out as she jumps from the top of a car in an aerial assault. Jace uses her inability to dodge to summon a demonic fist and knock her back to the ground. Sasha effortlessly slices the demon fist in half in one blow and thrusts her other hand forward in an attempt to grab him. Though he's about five feet away from her, he's unnaturally jerked downward towards her glowing knuckles. A split second before they reach his face, a metal staff appears in his hand, and he swiftly swings it just in time to block. Now back on the ground, he turns and looks at a beaming Kam, who gives him a small nod. Jace gracefully twirls the staff around a few times before sending it flying straight towards Sasha. Sasha quickly sidesteps the incoming staff, and while twisting her hands to match its rotation, she grabs it out of the air and spins back around, facing Jace with a smirk. By the time Sasha realizes he's nowhere in sight, Jace is already mid-way through performing a side aerial as he effortlessly yanks the staff out of her hands. He follows up by striking her back with both ends of the staff and finishes with a powerful leg sweep as soon as he lands. With her face now colored a fiery red, she ferociously bangs on the ground. sending a large surge of energy crashing towards him. Jace is sent soaring backwards, slamming into a nearby car. While groaning in pain, he quickly waves his hand, and a shadow arises from behind, grabbing both of Sasha's arms. She breaks away in an instant with a backflip right over the ghoul. She then splits it in half with a kick. Another figure suddenly glides behind her and slashes her side, moving in complete and utter silence.

"It's about time I cut in on this dance," Kam says with cold eyes. Now down on one knee, Sasha grabs her side, shrieking in pain. She looks down at her hands and notices her weapons are missing.

"No, my knuckles! Where are my cursed kn– AH!" She suddenly bellows out in pain while gripping her head with both hands. "What is, WHAT IS THIS!" she cries out in between breaths. Small tremors coming from the ground cause Kam to look around in confusion. Each weapon that had been used in battle was now violently rattling on the ground, slowly being lured in by Sasha's endless screams. For a brief moment, she seems to have her own gravitational pull. Her wild shrieks suddenly turn into a loud cackles as she's now back on her feet laughing senselessly. It's not long before she's grabbed from behind and thrown headfirst into the pavement. On the opposite end of her raised arm with one hand pushing down on her face is an exasperated Wade, just barely making it in time to subdue the crafty opponent.

"One move, and I'll break this arm in three places," he warns.

"Finally the fearless leader shows his face," she replies joyously.

"I would ask what the point of all this is, but I'd rather see for myself," Wade asserts before prying into her subconscious. "I see you've done some rather extensive research on us. To tell you the truth, I'm almost flattered. Apparently you needed our help chasing fairy tales. Even so this man you've spent so much time searching for, what does he mean to you? I've come across a name like this myself but….the only thing I've learned about this man is that he's a tree you shouldn't dare bark up. That it's more likely that HE will find YOU," Wade forewarns before setting her arm down.

"Well you could've asked for our help from the jump, but instead you just tried to Spartan kick us," Jace interrupts.

"Yeah, there's definitely better ways to ask for help. Why do you want us to hunt this man down so badly?" Kam asks.

"Because he's killing off all the good material! One day you hear about a man that can walk on walls, the next day he just disappears without a trace. Just a waste of views!" Sasha openly complains. "But you three must be an anomaly or something. You do all this vigilante work around here and yet you're still allowed to live. Off that fact alone, I figured all of the people like you were a force to be reckoned with," she continues to explain.

"So you're just a fan?" Kam angrily asks. She suddenly smiles ear to ear upon hearing this.

"Of course I am! Seeing the handsome Hero Trinity in action just confirmed it even more! I'm sure we've made enough noise today to catch his attention. Now it's only a matter of time before we all get see the fight of the century!" Sasha shouts, pumping her fist in the air. "Alright, she's clearly a basket case; let's just send fan girl on her way," Wade decides.

"Send her on her way? To where, jail?" Kam asks with his brow raised.

"Now wait a minute, she did say we were handsome though. Let's just let her slide and call this a workout," Jace chimes in.

"A what? Do you not see what she did to the city? She put you through a whole car, my guy!" Kam refutes.

Taking advantage of the ensuing chaos, Jace turns toward Sasha and whispers, "You might wanna get out of here before this gets ugly." She quietly slips away from the rowdy trio but not before blowing Jace a seductive kiss. Just a few miles away, real crime is afoot. Dead in the center of a shabby apartment complex is a large circle comprised of traumatized civilians, dutiful policemen, and endless lines of yellow tape encasing the area. Looking past the mortified crowd, you can see a forensics team finishing the chalk outline of a small body that had been burnt to a crisp.

"We got a positive ID on the body, sir. Josephine Hernandez," a detective reports. An imposing man is standing over the charred body with his arms folded. His most notable feature, other than his commanding presence is in his attire. Sporting a long black overcoat, a tactical chest rig, and a Glock 22 on his waist, you can tell this was a man who has been to war. Only desperate times call for a man of this caliber, in a place where crime never stops and maniacs never sleep.

Chapter 6: A Silent Farewell

"What happened here? We can see the smoke all the way from Holland Central," Kam asks as he and Jace arrive on the scene. They get stopped as soon as they're about to cross over the yellow tape.

"I'm not inclined to disclose that information," an imposing man in a long black coat replies.

"You don't understand. I need to make sure this isn't what I think this is. It's personal," Kam asserts.

"Personal? That was your first mistake," the man remarks.

"We don't make mistakes, we clean them up," Kam states with confidence.

"Just go home, kids, the whole city's been on edge and the last thing we need is trouble from a bunch of self-righteous punks who don't know their place," the man firmly commands. "You really think you're in a position to underestimate me?" Jace jumps in wearing a cold-blooded expression.

"Let's be real, you're not stopping us from crossing that line unless you got something more powerful than that Glock 22 on your hip. Like I said, I need to see what this is," Kam demands with unyielding resolve.

"You mean who this is?! Huh? The minute you cross that line, you get the privilege of explaining to their family which end is which. There will never, and I mean NEVER, be a day where you're used to seeing things like this! The look on these peoples' faces never change, the suffering never ends, and the crime never stops," the man angrily retorts.

"You think we don't understand suffering?! We're no stranger to pain ourselves. After the Pembrooke explosion, my dad couldn't even look at himself in the mirror for a second without being thrown into a padded room. Our brother is somewhere out here risking his life as we speak, and all we can do is have faith he'll come back safe," Jace states with a sharp glare. A few onlookers can be seen sneaking glances at the three bickering men. Standing amongst the crowd is a small Hispanic woman in a gray overcoat with her hands inside her pockets. Though there's a few teary-eyed witnesses in the crowd, her face seems the most sorrowful of all.

"Were you close to the victim?" a man leans in and asks.

"No, but I saw her pretty face on top of the building, and it reminded me of somebody I know. She was a real piece of work that one. So much talent with nothing to show for it," the woman laughs to herself as a stream of tears begin to fall from her eyes.

"Seems to me that this was a suicide. It's possible that in her last moments this poor girl shared your exact thoughts. Though I would hate to think that's the case," the man ponders.

"To be honest, I don't know if that makes me sad or happy. Damn that Josie for leaving me to continue on alone in a world like this," she scoffs with her head, now resting in her hands. "I'm sorry, but I don't believe they've released the identity of the victim to the public," the man states while turning to face the grief-stricken woman. Realizing her mistake, she removes her hands from her face and slowly starts to back away.

"Listen, Stephanie, don't make this harder than what it needs to be. Save us some time and turn yourself in, okay? I'm sure we can work this out somehow, there's always a way," the man reassures her in the middle of her attempt to slip away.

"Oh please, with all the bodies I've left in my wake? Unfortunately for me, I won't have that luxury," she replies just before breaking away from the crowd in a dead sprint.

"Sorry, brothers, looks like I'm handling this one on my own," Wade says to himself as he dashes ahead in pursuit of the lone Wake Sister.

"That guy was kind of a douche, right?" Jace snarls as he and Kam look over the incinerated corpse.

"Right! I don't know who he thought he was!" Kam shouts in agreement.

"The name's Frank Bishop," the man cuts in. "If you're gonna talk the talk, at least tell it to my face. And mention my name while you're at it, so I know just who it is you're barking at," he goes on pressing the issue.

"What, you didn't think we heard your heavy ass footsteps dragging behind us? We said it loud and clear the first time, so I didn't think I had to repeat myself," Kam snaps back. "Exactly, buzz cut, so how about we put our egos to the side and you tell us whether or not the body we see here is little Josie Hernandez," Jace demands.

"Yeah, it is. But how could you tell at first glance?" Frank asks, seemingly impressed. "We've been investigating reports on the Wake Sisters for a long time now and also looking through records of prime suspects fourteen-year-old Josephine Hernandez and twenty-eight-year-old Stephanie Hernandez," Kam explains.

"There had been rumors surfacing of the alleged victim suffering from physical and emotional abuse by her step-mother Stephanie. As soon as we seen this was a suicide, we automatically knew that this girl had had enough and decided to take her own life. To be forced into a life of crime at such a young age must've taken a heavy toll on her," Jace continues to further explain.

"Not to mention people in the crowd have been gossiping nonstop about a bright sapphire flame on top of the building. We've encountered supernatural occurrences such as this before at Saint Katherine's, in which we personally extinguished," Kam concludes.

"I see. Certainly a job well done connecting the dots. The question now is where's Stephanie Hernandez hiding after all this?" Frank inquires while putting his hand to his chin.

"If she's smart, she'd be far away from here," Jace states as the three men watch the coroner zip up the body of the deceased Wake Sister.

"Oh my gosh, a woman's being attacked!" shouts one of the bystanders in the crowd. Hearing this automatically sends the people into a state of panic.

"Someone stop him!"

"He's folded her hands so she can't escape!"

"Is he really doing something this vulgar in public?!" The people continue to cry out, but nobody steps in to help. With Stephanie now subdued, Wade demands an officer come forward and arrest her.

"This is the leader of the Wake Sisters! Put the pitchforks away and quit it with the mob mentality!" Wade barks.

"I guess even the wildest fires eventually get snuffed out," Stephanie comments as an officer finally arrives to seal her fate.

"Wow, maybe it's safe to say not all heroes wear capes," Jace jokes. Kam barely manages to keep his composure intact as he joins in on the applauding crowd with a sly smirk. "It was a clear case of Stockholm Syndrome. By the time she came to her senses, she felt like she had nowhere else to go, so she took matters into her own hands. If only she knew how many people out there would be willing to help her," Wade reports to Frank.

"I feel exactly the same way. It killed me to see it end like this," Jace responds in agreement.

"Nice work, and good job to you gentleman as well. Maybe civilians and heroes do work well together," Frank nods at the two masked men before he turns towards Wade with a salute. In order to keep his secret identity hidden, Wade is the first to leave the scene. He tightly grips his dog-tags as he reflects on the traumatic events of the day. The allure of flames is a double-edged sword. Not everything that looks good is good for you. With crime at an all-time low, the Hero Trinity spend the next few days relaxing in the comfort of their own home. The 56,000 square-foot mansion in Pearl's Gate was more than enough space for the boys to stretch their legs, yet they always find themselves gravitating to a particular building. The guest house turned training facility was more like home to them than any other part of the enormous Holland Estate. As soon as you set foot inside, you automatically think to take off your shoes. In this Japanese-Style space, Brazilian Cherry hardwood floors dance around green tatami mats, and along the walls are dozens of various weapons. Sai, Nunchaku, Bo staffs, lances, battles axes, maces, hook swords, katanas, and just about any other melee weapon you can dream of envelope the room. Looking past the entrance of the Trinity Dojo, there are three more rooms all designed for a specific purpose. A meditation chamber, lounge, and library provide the young heroes with everything they could ever need to hone their skills. Speaking of which, in the middle of the dojo sitting in seiza is Kam and Wade polishing their weapons in silence. Jace and Joe are biding their time in the lounge glued to the "must-see" wrestling event on TV.

"I think we should start teaching Joe how to protect himself. Maybe he should learn different fighting styles from all of us. What do you think?" Wade suddenly asks, breaking the silence.

"I agree. Jace should teach him the art of axe fighting and maybe even Taekwondo. With his long arms, he might be perfect for melee," Kam points out.

"Well then it's settled. To be honest, I've been planning this for a while; I'm already a few steps ahead. That trip to the bank was to finalize all of the paperwork for us to have a new training facility. I went ahead and bought a building right across the street from the abandoned church, but listen to this. I discovered a sub level secretly built in by a deranged conspiracy theorist who was adamant on preparing for the day the whole world will be enshrouded in darkness," he proceeds to disclose to Kam.

"That's amazing, bro. No surprise you had a bigger plan all along," Kam praises. He follows up by asking, "What else are you trying to accomplish by taking Joe under our wing?" "Sasha and now possibly Frank knowing our identities puts us at a huge risk, so even if we mask up, Joe can't," Wade immediately answers.

"Well then maybe the masks are useless. If the people begin to find out who we are, then it's possible that we can become bigger heroes than Prime ever was. We should be recognized by the world for our achievements. Besides, with our strength televised, we wouldn't be taken lightly regardless," Kam strongly states.

Wade calmly refutes with, "There's a thin line between the person we are meant to be and who we pretend to be. Even Prime wears a mask, what we know of him is just the face he puts on before he first walks out of the house. At the end of the day, we don't know what type of man he is behind closed doors."

"I see your point, but I still have my doubts," Kam admits.

"I expect no less from Kam the rational," Wade says with a pat on the shoulder. "Let me tell you the story of a man I once knew," he begins to narrate. "When he was thirteen, the T36 Virus plagued the world, and he lost both his parents. Him and his little sister went to live with their grandmother, who he loved the most in the whole world. One day his grandma falls terribly ill from the virus and is bedridden. A few days later, he sneaks into his grandmother's room in the dead of night to bring her her favorite snack and discovers his sister smothering her with a pillow. She claims that her grandmother begged her to do it and wouldn't stop asking, so she had no choice, there was no other way. His sister was immediately sent to a psychiatric hospital and him an orphanage. The man spent most of his life alone but was able to talk to his sister over the phone twice a week. Besides his classmate, who he would go out for drinks with every now and then, the only light in his life was his girlfriend who was mute. On the first night of her moving in, his home was raided by an armed assailant. He managed to push his girlfriend out of the way of an incoming bullet, but she falls and cracks her head, dying on impact. The robber then got spooked and shot the man in the head. The man managed to jam a rod into the robber's skull just before he lost consciousness. Upon awaking at the hospital, he didn't remember a single thing about himself, but hearing from the doctors that everybody he ever loved was taken away from him, his mind was sent into a void he couldn't escape. A few weeks later, he ended up murdering his classmates, college professor, and everybody else he held dear. For the final act, he was planning to finish his sister off, but I ran into him at the psychiatric hospital just before he couldn't. He told me that he could figure out why he was there in the first place, so I restored all of his memories starting with the one he cherished most. It was of his sister and his grandmother going out for Halloween, despite his parents' wishes. They merrily walked the streets wearing the homemade costumes she sewed for them. He was so happy that even a mouth full of cavities wouldn't have stopped that smile. The last words he spoke to me were, 'I guess I needed somebody to blame for all this and I chose me.'"

"The moral of the story is that losing his identity was like losing the mask he used to keep his demons in check. In reality he died the day his grandmother did. The only thing left of his conscience was rage, pain, and trauma. He went on a rampage, completely acting on emotion, and decided to change fate in the most despicable way, by killing the rest of his past with his own hands. He willingly let himself be guided by his malevolent self because deep down he knew this was always a part of him. He atoned for his sins then and there, turning himself in having come to terms with his sadistic side. Just remember, Kam, when you're a hero, you need to always be sure of who you are. That mask, and the ones donning it with you, are a reminder of just that. Every single person in this world needs a mask, and ours we wear with pride. The only thing we should ever be scared to lose sight of is ourselves. We have no choice but to keep our demons in check," he concludes with a powerful message. Kam just sits there in awe, reflecting on Wade's words.

Upon coming to a realization, Kam suddenly asks, "There's only one thing I don't get. Why were you at a psychiatric hospital to begin with?...."

"Yo!" Jace suddenly comes bursting out of the room howling. "Kam, you just missed ya boy do his famous spear!" he says before he's suddenly tackled by Joe. Wade proceeds to tackle Kam off-guard, and the boys all fall on the mats, holding their stomachs in laughter.

"It's fine, bro. I'm glad you at least recorded it. You did record it, right?" Kam asks with a worrisome expression. Suddenly it seemed like half the laughter in the room had died down.

Chapter 7: Brothers in Arms

You can travel to any place in time and see that death nor poverty is ever one to play favorites. With this being said, the Eastside of Sapphire City is certainly no exception. Somewhere in the trenches lurking where the homeless seek solace lies a ragtag group of troublemakers disturbing the tiny shred of peace they've come to know. A timid beggar is groveling at the feet of a brawny Mexican man with a bulging gut and bald patches blotted all over his head. Beside him are three other men with matching flaming skull tattoos, leather vests, and menacing smiles.

"Please, gentlemen, just leave me alone. I just want to eat in peace," the beggar pleads. "Eat? Now how you gonna do that without my help, uh….Sergeant Bison? I just came to pay my dues to the men and women who fought so hard for this country," the man replies as he makes out a name on the beggars tattered jacket.

"Did he say gentleman? What, you think you're better than us cuz you use manners, Mr. Bison? Don't forget where you are, old man; you're washed up," says one of the other men. He has a look of utter disgust on his face as he turns around and walks away while combing his fingers through his mohawk. The old man is now quaking in fear for he realizes that their wicked games may never end.

"Damn, old timer, keep your hands up. The Parkinson's can't be that bad," one of them says as he drops pennies into his hand one by one. The words of this slender skeleton of a man leave the group roaring with laughter.

"Thank you for the change good, sirs," Mr. Bison mumbles before turning around to finish his meal.

"Hey, who gave you permission to turn your back on me?" a bald man with large gauges in his ears barks. Seething with anger, he points a nine milimeter at the back of Mr. Bison's skull.

"Oh God, please don't! Please!" Mr. Bison desperately pleads with his hands up.

"I see you scum like to play with guns, how 'bout you take this on for size?" a masked man interrupts. One look at this man, and you can tell that he was the one in control. Surprisingly enough in his hand was a M134 mini-gun ready to fire more a minute than an auctioneer on his first day.

"Welp we missed a whole comedy film just to turn around and see a Western. I guess you can say it's a fair trade-off," Jace jokes with his shoulders shrugged.

"More like standoff. The weapon is a little excessive, but in this case I don't blame him," Wade murmurs out the corner of his mouth.

"Alright I'll take bowl cut and rough patch," Jace decides.

"I guess that just leaves rock band," Kam says joining in on the fun. "What? They all look like rock band, you mean mini moha–"

"Kam? Jace?" Wade starts to complain but is caught completely off guard upon hearing his brother's identities revealed. Kam and Jace both greet the mini mohawk man with an icy glare. The bitter looks on their faces slowly fade as they realize who it is they're staring at. "Princeton?!!" Kam blurts out in complete shock.

"No, it can't be," Jace responds in disbelief. "I haven't seen you since you got rejected at the Winter Formal. This who you been running with?" Jace asks in ridicule.

"I can't believe you turned out this way. What would Cheyenne and Ashley think?" Kam follows up as the two openly express their disappointment.

"What can I say? Not everybody gets to be adopted by a rich white family," a sour-faced Princeton replies.

"And not everybody's parents were taken away right before their eyes," Wade steps up in defense.

"How did you even find us vatos?" Rough Patch chimes in.

"You terrorized a whole alley full of homeless men and women without expecting a single one to run and ask for help? Foolish," Wade bitterly states. The four men don't hesitate to let out a small snicker upon hearing this.

"I mean who was gonna believe a bunch of drunks and washed up vets anyway?" Bowl Cut blurts out.

"We would. And this little charade ends here," Wade asserts with a cold-blooded look in his eyes.

"Finally something we both agree on. I'm ready to paint the walls with some brains!" the bald one shouts as he slams the old man into the brick wall and cocks back his gun.

"Make another move like that, and I start shaving heads!" Kam warns while having his mini-gun around.

"Oh, I'm counting on it!" the bald man retorts, wearing a sadistic smile as he presses the gun further into the man's skull. With this Wade finally decides to give the command.

"He goes first. Kam, take out his legs." He didn't even get a chance to finish his sentence before Kam sends an onslaught of bullets raining down. The bony man with the bowl cut immediately jumps into the line of fire with his mouth outstretched, like a hippopotamus. Six thousand rounds per minute seems like Sunday brunch to him as he ingests each bullet with relative ease.

"My hunger is never satisfied," he states while rubbing his stomach. Kam proceeds to throw his minigun on the ground, but just before it sinks down, a pillar shoots out from the brick wall. Bowl Cut is forcefully slammed straight through the next abandoned building over. As soon as Kam sees a shadow attempting to carry the homeless man to safety, he starts to run straight for the armed man ahead of him.

"Ha, think I didn't see that coming?" the bald man gloats before firing a shot right into the homeless man's temple.

"No!" the boys shout in unison as they see the life entrusted to them fade away before their eyes.

Princeton suddenly calls out to the boys in their moment of sorrow, "Why the long face? We spared him a life of poverty."

"Yeah, now you don't have to donate ten cents a day," Rough Patch says with a loud cackle.

"Weakness should never be accepted in this world. Just looking at him was a disgrace," the bald man remarks with his face crumpled up. Wade immediately takes a step forward with his fists clenched so hard, his knuckles turn white.

"Do you even understand how hard this man fought for this country? For you? You take his life over a petty squabble like this, and the first look I see on your face is disgust? You deserve no mercy!" he states with strong conviction.

"Damn right we took his miserable life, and you better remember the names of the ones who did it. We're The Sunken Four," the bald man answers. They then begin to introduce themselves, starting with their despicable leader.

"The name's Soul."

"I'm Wraith."

"Scythe here."

"And I'm Reap– ah!" A shadow shuriken suddenly rips through the air, nearly taking an ear off.

"That's it! Jace is mine; everybody, get back! I'm gonna shut that mouth up once and for all!" Princeton yells out.

"Why don't we all take this to the streets, then I'm sure you want a little more breathing room than this," Jace responds as he turns around and walks away. Princeton follows suit and heads out of the alleyway, casually walking on the side of the building walls with his hands in his pockets. Seeing this causes Wade to grab Jace and warn him to be careful.

"Skin em' alive," Kam calls out to them before they vanish out of sight.

"Scythe, you take the one who had that minigun. If he's lucky, the last person he'll ever see will be you and not me," Soul commands with a malicious grin.

"I guess I got the pretty white boy then," Wraith says while scratching at the little spots of hair on his head.

"We'll take you all on two versus three, I don't know why you thought you get to dictate this fight," Kam snaps. Ignoring his demands, Wraith and Scythe suddenly rush in on the attack with Soul sitting back, keeping a watchful eye.

"Do it now, Wraith!" Scythe shouts as he closes in on Kam. As he's running towards him, his eyes shift from focused to deranged with each step. You can see the veins in his arms and forehead nearly bursting out, and he begins to foam at the mouth like a rabid animal. A pair of Herculean stone golems with Olmec heads quickly emerge from the ground to block their path. The illusion of protection is shattered in an instant as Scythe leaps up in the air, chomping its head clean off. The other golem is quickly laid to rest by Wraith, who nearly disintegrates it with a single punch. He appears to be in a similar state as Scythe with bulging veins and bloodshot eyes, however, his concentration seems to be more prominent than his partner's.

"I guess these guys are more bite than bark," Kam mutters as he takes a fighting stance. "Well let's see if all dogs do go to heaven," Wade replies, cracking his knuckles.

"I gotta say, I don't like that look in your eyes, Prince," Jace states as they face off in front of a condemned residential building.

"Oh, trust me, Jace, with Wraith giving me this much of a power boost, I oughta see plenty of fear on that smug little face of yours," Princeton states with confidence. Jace begins by running in with a flying kick, but the closer it gets to Princeton, the slower his momentum gets until he's completely frozen in the air. Princeton walks around Jace in a full circle, laughing hysterically the whole time he's observing him. By the time Jace is able to move again, he's falling into a powerful uppercut that puts him flat on his back.

"Yeah, you definitely hit like a Princeton," Jace jokes while rubbing his jaw.

"GR, AH! You bastard! See if you're still laughing after this!" Princeton roars as he sprints towards Jace. Before he can react, Princeton grabs Jace and springs into the air, jumping halfway up a ten-story building in a single leap. By the time Princeton is soaring through the air, Kam and Wade are already bombarding their opponents with lethal strikes from their bladed weapons. With his twin lion swords in hand, Wade slashes vigorously at Wraith, keeping him on the defensive. Kam is now equipped with an anelace dagger, in which he uses to slash various weak points of Scythe's body. He twirls around and slashes the back of both of his knees, forcing him to the ground.

"Wraith, I need MORE!" he screams out in a fit of rage. A few seconds later, Scythe's whole body starts to quiver and turn a dangerous red as if his fury had sprang to life.

"Careful, Wraith, in about three seconds he's about to grab your arm and rip straight through your side," their leader Soul unexpectedly warns. Hearing this causes Scythe to dart towards Wade on all fours. He immediately chomps down on both of the swords in Wade's hands, leaving nothing but the hilt. Wade forces him back with a push, but again he lunges at him in an attempt to finish him off while he's defenseless. All of a sudden, two long blades appear from the broken hilts as Kam comes in for the save. However, this save seems to be in vain for the swords are once again ground to a pulp by Scythe's seemingly indestructible jaws. Just as he's about to tear through Wade's face, a bull whip constricts his partner's neck and forcefully drags him back. The brutal sound of Wraith gasping for air causes Scythe to curiously look back. As soon as he turns back around to finish Wade off, his skull is smashed between two sword hilts. He's left sprawling on the ground as Wade dashes towards the asphyxiating Wraith and knocks what little air he had left out of him with a powerful dropkick.

"Sorry, didn't mean to bring the fight your way. I won't let him out of my sight again," Kam says as he coats his arms and legs with metal guards. He then walks up to the recovering Scythe once again, taking a battle stance.

"Didn't anybody tell you that I'm my brother's keeper?" he asks wearing his infamous smirk. Miraculously poised halfway up a ten-story building in an intense standoff is Princeton and Jace. The first to make a move is Princeton, who uses his feet to smash a window in. Not even a single shard of glass falls on impact, but instead they all float upward and swarm around him. With a wave of his hand, dozens of fragments are sent spiraling towards Jace. About half of the pieces of glass fall to the ground before reaching him, and the rest are absorbed into a large ball of darkness and sent back at Princeton. In a near miss, Princeton quickly ducks to avoid the returning glass.

"Why would some of them fall down but not all? He must be manipulating his own personal gravity, but maybe keeping me planted here as well is too much of a strain. I'm assuming he can only control gravitational fields within a small radius, but even that must be limited if he has to worry about keeping us both balanced up here. Just as I thought, every great power has a weakness," Jace thinks to himself as he looks to gain the upper hand. "I think I got you figured out, Prince," he calls out with a confident smile.

"My name is Reaper!" Princeton shouts, now boiling with rage. He sends another wave of glass shards flying, but Jace quickly side flips to evade. Princeton attempts to run towards him, but both of his legs are mounted down by a pair of smoky hands. Suddenly a shroud of darkness begins to pour in, violently rotating in a whirlwind. A shadow tornado starts to accumulate, rapidly spinning along the building and engulfing Princeton in its circulation as he's whipped around relentlessly. The very glass that he commanded to slice through Jace is now caught in the vortex, picking his flesh apart little by little. Jace matches the movement of his own creation as he flies in to finish him off with a tornado kick. Nearly unconscious Princeton uses the last of his strength to break his fall as he comes crashing down. As Jace lands, he loses his center of gravity and is now sliding down the building at breakneck speed. Just before he smacks the ground, he creates a smoky hand that pops out the side of the building. At the last minute, he quickly grabs hold of it, narrowly saving his own skin. He kicks off of the building in a backflip, landing just in time to hear Kam's dire warning.

"Stand down, it's over! You lost!" Kam shouts at an out of control Scythe who is ceaselessly foaming at the mouth. At this point, Kam has him on the ropes and is now pinning him down to the ground. His warning falls on deaf ears as an unrelenting bloodlust seems to shake the core of Scythe's very being. He continues to bite and gnaw away at Kam's metal guards, showing no signs of surrender. Kam continues to materialize layer after layer of armor, but it's being chewed away by the second in a never-ending cycle.

"I said SURRENDER!" Kam yells out in a final attempt to bring him to his senses. "AH!" Kam suddenly screams out, trying to find the resolve to do what must be done. Jace unexpectedly steps in, throwing two shadow shuriken dead in the center of his skull, leaving his body limp. Just as Kam is about to rise up, Scythe suddenly lunges in for a final bite. His throat is forcibly crushed under the weight of Kam's mighty elbow thrust. Kam stands over the body with a look that's seemingly devoid of all emotion. It was then when he truly began to question whether life was really precious or just another candle waiting to be blown out.

Chapter 8: I Bet You Didn't See That Coming

"Kam! Kam!" Wade shouts desperately in an attempt to bring him back to reality. Kam shakes his head violently, trying to find himself again. However, the disdainful words coming from his opponent only add fuel to the fire.

"I see you've finally dealt with my pet. Now it's time for the owner to clean up his dog's mess," Soul says as he draws a second nine milimeter from his hip. "Wraith, now!" he commands with a snap. Now just as unhinged as his opponents, Kam starts to rush in with bloodlust eyes. Soul fires his gun, but Jace quickly casts a shadow to absorb the bullets.

"Kam, get your head in the game!" Wade yells at him from a distance while he continues to deal with Wraith. Snapping back to his senses, Kam pulls out a new mini gun and fires at Soul, who manages to dodge the first few bullets and find cover before all hell breaks loose. "You're gonna have to do better than that! I saw that coming from a mile away!" he boasts. He's now sweating profusely with veins popping out all over his shiny head and crazed eyes.

"I wouldn't go getting too ahead of myself if I were you," Jace replies as he's now looming over Soul. He sends him flying forward with a kick, but he quickly rolls over in the opposite direction, evading before he can be crushed beneath Kam's feet. He knocks the minigun out of Kam's hands, and it slides all the way towards Wade and Wraith. Just in the nick of time, Wade jumps over the minigun while throwing a flash kick, knocking Wraith face first into the barrel. Wraith immediately bounces back up in an angry screech. His raw anger spread like a contagion, for Soul also began to psyche out in that exact same moment. The first thing he squeezes is his head, next the trigger. He attempts to catch Jace off guard with a shot to the chest, but Kam steps in before he has the chance. He stomps the ground, causing it to ripple like rocks skipping through a lake, forcing Jace to tumble down to the ground kissing gravel.

"Ah, what the hell?!" he cries out.

"Well it was worth a shot," Soul says as the bullets narrowly miss its target.

"Left, right, right, left, headbutt. This guy's moves are so linear, it's almost pitiful to watch," Wade whispers as he easily predicts all of Wraith's movements. "Time to end this," he asserts. He suddenly ducks down and grabs a fresh pair of swords as they emerge from the ground. He slashes the back of both of Wraith's shins, bringing him to his knees for he's no longer able to stand. Next he goes for his midsection, carving an X into his abdomen with two diagonal strikes. Wraith is then completely folded by an axe kick to the chest. The fight ends with a skewer as Wade thrushes his swords into each arm, finishing him off. In the midst of Wade's triumph, it seems Kam has come to a realization.

"I think I got this guy figured out Jace. I can handle this one alone," Kam says.

"By yourself? Ha, don't make me laugh, kid," Soul retorts.

"Give 'em hell with the Kam-Fu," Jace calls out before heading back towards the rundown building where Princeton awaits.

"Shouldn't have given me time to reload," Soul says as he fires six rounds at point blank range. Two stone golems manage to emerge just in time to take most of the damage, but the last round hits Kam straight in the chest, causing him to stagger back.

"Damn, that's hot! It's been a while since I been shot; I almost forgot how that felt," Kam jests while swiping the smoking hollow tip from his chest. He sends a shuriken flying at his throat in retaliation, but Soul snaps his head to the side, dodging just in time. Immediately after Soul dodges, Kam jerks his hand back in a yanking motion, and the shuriken comes flying back, spinning twice as fast. Soul quickly ducks, but it's not enough to stop the shuriken from partially tearing through his shoulder. He's brought down to his knees from the shock. Just before he rises up again, a cloud of dust is flung into his eyes, and his face is met with a vicious left hook from Wade.

"And that confirms it," Kam notes as his eyes narrow.

"Took you long enough to figure it out," Wade says panting. "Let's finish him o–" Wade starts to say, but his air supply is suddenly cut off. Wraith is now standing behind him with earphones around his neck, choking him with a manic smile on his face. He forces Wraith back with a powerful head butt, followed by an elbow to the rib cage.

"Did you….did you really lacerate the tendons in both of your arms just to rip through the blades?" Wade asks in between breaths.

"No pain, no gain," Wraith replies while cracking his neck.

"I guess I'll entertain you till your blood runs dry," Wade whispers to himself with his guard now up. Several yards away, looking up at a completely enraged Princeton, is a beaming Jace.

"So should I take the elevator or?" he jokingly asks.

"By all means," Princeton replies, motioning his hand upwards. Jace then gathers himself, and with a running start, he dashes up the building. "Oops," Princeton blurts out with his shoulders shrugged. A little more than halfway up the building, Jace suddenly loses his footing and comes tumbling down. In the first couple of seconds, he completely loses his nerve and starts failing his arms in desperation. In the next moment, he takes a deep breath and closes his eyes, accepting his fate. He opens his eyes to find himself surrounded in complete nothingness, yet somehow still falling. By the time he blinks again, he still seems to be falling, but beneath him lies an unsuspecting Princeton about to be mauled down. Jace uses his momentum to his advantage as he twists in the air and nearly caves Princeton's back in with a butterfly kick. Princeton is immediately sent spiraling down the building, spitting up blood. Now free-falling, Jace once again shuts his eyes and descends into a smoky portal. He comes back out just a few feet above the ground as he smacks into the concrete. This automatically causes the others to glance between a wincing Jace on the ground and a dry heaving Princeton, barely clinging onto the building above.

"Hmph?" Kam says as he stares at Jace in confusion.

"Hm!" Jace replies while tracing his finger in a circle. Coming to an understanding, Kam starts to slowly pedal backwards. A few steps in, he's engulfed in black smoke and reappears running straight at Princeton with momentum alone carrying him downward. He quickly throws two kunai, and mid-way through the air, they start to miraculously multiply. Over a dozen kunai are then sent crashing into all of the glass surrounding Princeton.

"Ha, at this point you're just making this easy for me," Princeton boasts as he sends an array of fallen shards at Kam. Before all of the glass can reach him, Kam has already been transported back to the ground. A couple yards away, Soul is seen frantically wriggling around trying to free himself from the grasp of two shadow ghouls pinning him down. He just barely manages to fire a few shots at an incoming Jace, but he disappears right before they could reach him.

"Slippery bastard," Souls says. He's then suddenly grabbed from behind and slammed on his back by a crushing suplex from Kam. Before he can even decipher the pain, Kam rolls on top of Soul and blitzes him with a barrage of punches. By the next time we see Jace, he's looking up at Princeton, but this time he greets him with a surprise. Princeton's eyes slowly widen as he desperately ducks for cover from the onslaught of bullets dumping at him from the mini-gun. He jumps inside of the building, seeking shelter until the shooting stops. Every which way, debris is endlessly hailing down like a winter shower as Jace is tearing down walls, leaving him with no place to hide.

"Damn, I'm out of ammo! And I'm about to be out of options, too," Jace complains. "Sounds like it's my turn to play," Princeton says, popping his head back out. He slowly raises his hands in a dramatic fashion, but nothing seems to follow this notion. Kam's earlier attack caused him to send all of the broken glass out of his range. Looking around in hysteria, Princeton begins to panic. This feeling doesn't last long for he's suddenly bombarded by a slew of shadow bullets.

"You really think I would tell someone I was out of options? Never trust the enemy, princess!" Jace shouts out from below. Before Princeton can fully discern what pieces were suddenly missing from his body, black smoke starts to rapidly pour out from his calf all the way to his side. He begins to fall down the building unconscious. His leg is severed from his body as he makes his way down, leaving only three limbs to break his fall. Now drenching his blood all over the street, Wraith is desperately crying out while being choked from behind by Wade.

"Kam! Incoming!" he shouts before taking a few steps back. With a running start, he dropkicks him in the back, knocking him towards Kam with unrelenting force.

"I guess the only way to put these guys down is to actually put them down," Kam says to himself. He then hastily jumps from on top of Soul to catch Wraith by the shoulders and toss him twenty yards in a single throw. "Catch!" he shouts as Wrath is forcefully slammed into the plunging Princeton, and they both crash into the abandoned building. The concussive force renders them both barely clinging to life as they bathe the street in blood. Soul slowly begins to stagger back on his feet, watching in horror as his comrades paint the city like a mural. He starts to mutter something, but the words fail to reach the Hero Trinity. Instead he tries to reach for his gun, but before he gets the chance, a hand pierces right through his stomach, and he immediately starts choking on his own blood.

"I bet you didn't see that coming," a mysterious voice blurts out. He slowly turns around to look his killer in the eyes, but they are forcefully closed shut as he slides down the arm of the mysterious murderer.

"What's the point of seeing into the future if you can't even watch your own back? What a shame," Alias says as she shakes the blood off of her arm.

"Wait, were you watching us this whole time?" Wade asks with a puzzled look.

"Of course I was, Mr. Holland. It's not every day that I get to witness a battle between two deadly sins and two new gens," Alias continues. The now utterly exhausted Kam and Jace look over at each other as they start to put together who Alias is hinting at.

"What do you know about us?" Kam decides to ask.

"I know that since that tragic day at Pembrooke you were forcibly awakened. It was then that you became an anomaly, something this millennia has barely seen the likes of," she explains. As she says this, she turns and looks at Princeton and Wraith. "There's no point of playing dead when I can make your wish a reality," Alias calls out to the boys. She then grabs Soul's guns from his waist and sinks two bullets into the skulls of Wraith and their old friend Princeton.
"Why would you do that!" Kam screams out.

"Answer him!" Jace exclaims.

"The biggest fault in having power is the illusion that it is absolute," Alias strongly states. Kam immediately rushes in to attack Alias, but Wade yells for him to stop for he notices the presence of others. Jace runs to cover Kam's back, and Wade runs to deal with John, who had been standing on the sidelines until now.

"Stay sharp, guys, these two are clearly more dangerous than anything we've ever faced!" Wade warns as the two zip past him.

"More than you know," John states. He deploys a small ensemble of undead who simultaneously rush at Wade.

"No way those are real zombies!" Jace shouts in bewilderment. Wade prepares himself to take on all fifteen zombies barehanded, but twin swords suddenly emerge from the ground with signature black and gold lion heads decorating the hilt.

"Thanks, Kam, you're a lifesaver," Wade mumbles to himself. Jace and Kam decide to rush Alias in each direction but are laid down in an instant. As they drew near, Alias leapt in the air, wrapping both their necks around her arms and legs spinning them around like a power drill. "I wouldn't get back up if I were you," she warns them. The boys ignore her warning and begin to slowly rise up but are engulfed in the flames of two scorching fire blasts sent from Alias. Kam desperately struggles to get back on his feet but is immediately shot in the back, leaving both of the boys down for the count.

"I told you to stay down, pretty boy," she again warns. "You two, hold him down," she commands two zombies. A few heads roll over by Kam and Jace, causing them to look over at Wade standing his ground alone. Faced with eight zombies left, he takes them all down in under a minute. A lingering zombie suddenly rolls into a ball and rams into Wade's legs, striking him down. He drops his swords, and they are kicked out of his reach. The zombie then once again folds into a cannonball and attempts to crush Wade's skull with his supernatural speed. Wade quickly yells for Kam but instead of a weapon, a smoky portal appears in front of him, sending the incoming zombie ramming into a wall. He looks over to thank Jace, but to his horror, he's discovers Kam pinned to the ground unconscious. Just before he turns back around, a man in a black suit taps him on his shoulders and whispers "Boo" in his ear. With a mere mutter, a powerful shockwave blasts Wade back several yards, instantly taking him out. Given nothing but a small nod from John, three zombies come over to subdue him as instructed. Jace's screams finally reach Kam for he slowly comes to just in time to let himself free.

"AH!" Kam roars as metal spikes protrude from his back, plunging deep into the flesh of the undead. He jerks to the side, shoving the corpse off of him while acting on pure instinct. He runs up to rescue Wade but is choke slammed in the blink of an eye.

"I couldn't even follow her movements just then; what the hell is she?" Jace asks in shock.

"Number One, hold this one still! I want him to watch what happens next," Alias commands. The man in the black suit follows her orders with no hesitation and turns Kam's head towards Alias as she lies in wait. In that same moment, John Doe decides to personally join the fray.

He takes a knee and whispers to the captured Wade, "Be grateful, boy, there's no greater honor than a noble death. You've fought your fight; submit peacefully, and I'll make sure your final moments are blissful." Shortly after Alias also approaches with a wicked agenda. Wade's eyes begin to narrow as he prepares to gather his final words.

"Never forget this lesson, pretty boy. This is how you disassemble a team.

You cut off the head and watch the body squirm as their restless souls melt away," Alias looks directly in Kam's eyes and says.

Wade also takes a final glance at his beloved brothers before telling them: "I couldn't live with myself if I let you guys die before me. As a dead man's final wish, spare them, will you?" John squints his eyes as he gazes down upon him. "Tell Joe I'm sorry I couldn't make it to his graduation. Let Mom and Dad know they did a hell of a job raising us. I know that's a little basic, just spice it up a little for me. It's been an honor serving with you guys, I truly love you brothers." Alias then lifts up Wade's head and shows him to the two boys who are desperately struggling to get back up. Jace is frantically gnawing at the arm of the zombie holding him down, hoping to rip through enough cartilage to set him free. As she holds up his head, an icicle ever so slowly extends from her wrist, quietly sinking into Wade's neck. The life begins to fade from his eyes as blood spews from his collar like a geyser. Alias then walks up to the boys with a crazed look in her eyes, licking the blood off the icicle.

She heads over and leans in whispering, "Well, Jace, I would tell you to go see your father, but it looks like you get to see your mother's first." As she raises her hand, she hears footsteps as John walks away from the scene. The crazed look begins to disappear from her eyes, turning into a wry smile.

"Looks like you get to live another day. Don't worry, I won't leave without giving you boys a parting gift, that's just bad manners," she tells them. She gently kisses the top of their heads and walks off humming an eerie tune. As they fade off in the distance, Kam starts clawing at his eyes, drowning in unfathomable pain. Jace rolls around grabbing his chest and arms, screaming for his life. Kam is curled up rolling every which way while a myriad of shadows are dancing the Macabre inside his eyes. He keeps blinking in and out of existence with each passing moment. He lets out a huge roar as a dark humanoid dragon springs out from his chest. The beast shadow emerges, mimicking Kam's thunderous bellow, a roar like nothing this world has ever seen. Now stabilizing Kam staggers back up as the monstrous aura seeps back inside his body. Meanwhile Jace is on the ground mortified as he's being slowly entombed in gravel, buried alive by an uncontrollable power. He tries to fight it, but his arms are already trapped underneath. In a desperate attempt to escape certain death, golden gauntlet blades suddenly shoot out from his arms, and he breaks himself free by sheer force. He lets out an emphatic battle cry as he finally gains a slight grip on this new phenomenon. The boys then solemnly watch as Wade's lion swords sink into the ground before finally finding the strength to look over at his body. They gently wrap a scarf around his neck and carry him home in complete and utter silence. As of today, The Hero Trinity is no more.

Chapter 9: Everything's Alive

The hardest part about dealing with death is the toll it takes on your loved ones. This became woefully clear the moment Kam and Jace stepped foot back onto the compound. As Murphy's Law dared come into play, the two boys were immediately met at the gates by a disconcerted Joe. To say it looked like he had seen a ghost would be an understatement, for it would be more accurate to say it looked as if his heart had been shattered in pieces, leaving only one thing to fill the empty husk. Rage. His dear elder brother had just been laid on the ground before him dressed in hideous battle scars.

"No, no, no, no, this can't be real," Joe mumbles while unwrapping the scarf around Wade's neck.

"I'm so sorry, Joe. He wanted to let you know he's sorry he couldn't make it to your graduation," a teary-eyed Kam says through a raspy voice.

"He was fighting till his last breath like a true soldier," Jace adds.

"Soldiers are disposable, you know he was more than that. He was our brother," Joe replies with a cold glare.

"Of course, bro. And he always will be," Jace assures, but his words seem to fall on deaf ears.

"So what were you doing? Huh? Why is Kam struggling to even stay on his feet right now, yet compared to him, you seem just fine? What, were you just standing around cracking jokes while his throat was getting slit?!" Joe snaps.

"Oh, hell nah. You don't get to say that when you weren't out there! We ALL fought side by side till the end against things you couldn't even begin to comprehend! He gave his life to save us fr–"

"Oh my God, Wade?! WADE!" Jace's words were abruptly cut off by Mrs. Holland's screams. She rushes to Wade's side and pulls him to her chest, but the moment his lifeless arms dangle beneath her shoulders, she completely loses it. To the boys' surprise, Mr. Holland steps up from behind, laying a comforting hand on his wife's shoulders.

"We knew this could happen at any time, but to think this moment would actually come is unbearable. Still knowing he proudly gave his life for his brothers' sake is nothing short of admirable. We did a fine job raising him, Sue," Mr. Holland says, trying his best to console her as the tears stream from his eyes. Their father's words seem comforting, but in reality he was struggling to look anyone in the eye.

"I'm sorry, everyone, we did the best we could. I swear.." Kam cries out before collapsing from exhaustion. Catching a glimpse at his charred and battered back, Joe starts to take a few steps away in shock.

"Gashes? Burn marks? Bullets wounds? Who could've done all of this?" Joe asks, continuing to hound them with difficult questions.

"It…it was zombies," Jace answers with reluctance. His ridiculous response only adds fuel to the raging inferno rising inside of Joe.

"Wade's gone, Kam's practically on the brink of death, and you're STILL making jokes?! I should kill you myself!" Joe snarls while lunging at Jace. Jace's unbearable guilt leaves him unwilling to dodge, and he's clocked with the full force of a hook to the chin.

"Joseph you've done enough! You know they're out there day and night risking their lives! You have no right to chastise them! Think about how they feel! You have no idea how hard it is to have to lay their brother's body across their parents feet," Mrs. Holland suddenly shouts, immediately smoldering the wild fire that was Joe.

"Come on, Joe…it's me, man. Do you really believe I would just stand there watching our brother get killed and do nothing? Do I look unscathed to you? Does it look like I can stand just fine?! Look at me. LOOK AT ME!" Jace screams in agony as his knees fold and buckle to the ground.

"Joe, inside NOW!" Mr. Holland scolds. He then takes off his blazer and throws it over Wade's body. "He's already cold…" Mr. Holland murmurs as he wipes the tears off of his face. Hearing his father's words, Joe grits his teeth and reluctantly follows his command. Just before he reaches the door, he stops to speak the words that would haunt them for the rest of their lives. "You bastards killed Wade. You'll never be able to wash that blood off your hands," he asserts. Things haven't been the same for the Holland household since that fateful day. A week later, Kam and Jace are standing in front a desolate lot as they take on the world with a new agenda.

"Lemme ask you something, bro. Your power, is there any part of it that you miss?" Jace suddenly blurts out.

"Hm, that's a good question I'm almost scared to answer. At first I felt like I lost everything, but when reality kicks in, I remember that hell is real. We lost something more important than any of that, and I want a soul back in return. So I guess you can say maybe I'm too focused on Wade, or I wasn't as connected to them as I thought," Kam answers with a shrug. "Yeah, I was thinking the same thing. Taking something so powerful for granted is probably what hindered us from unlocking our full potential in the first place. Now because of that, losing powers isn't the only thing we gotta live with for the rest of our lives. But as many times as we fought or seen each other fight, we should get the hang of all this pretty quick. From now on, let's just take some time to really understand ourselves and what we can do," Jace states with strong conviction.

"Hmph, wishful thinking, bro, but I guess we have no choice. A bond so strong that I'm scared to lose it. That's the goal from now on," Kam decides with his fist clinched.

"By the way, uh….is this the place that's supposed to be ours?" Jace turns and asks.

"As far I know," Kam nonchalantly replies.

"Well did he at least leave us a key?" Jace jokes. Facing the two boys was a split-level brick building surrounded by nothing but dead trees and withered shrubs. Across the street is a large Basilica that had been long since condemned, marking them the only two buildings for miles that haven't been torn down or gentrified. What happened to catch their eyes wasn't the barren atmosphere, however, but the all too familiar black sign hanging from the double doors. "Discipline, huh? Talk about the ties that bind," Jace says before raising an axe to the door. With a single strike, he cuts down the lock and chains that had been wrapped around them. "Feels like home already," Kam mutters sarcastically.

"Home is family not a place," a cigar smoking man walks up and says.

"I thought I told you that you're gonna need more than that Glock 22 to put us down," Kam barks. As he says this, the man lets out a soft chuckle while taking a glimpse at the pistol tucked inside his black overcoat.

"Relax, gentleman. I'm here on behalf of our fallen comrade," Frank states. "Civilians and heroes really can work together. Believe it or not, I learned that from Wade," he continues. "You come up here talking like you knew Wade and you just expect us to take you at your word?!" Jace snaps.

"The fact that I even know this place exists should be proof enough. Who do you think gave him the idea?" Frank replies.

"And?" Kam rhetorically asks.

"And that's not the only thing I know. Wade used to perform plenty of miracles during his tour; he was certainly one hell of a doctor. He's told you about the killer amnesiac I presume?" Frank asks while inhaling a fresh puff.

"Alright, I understand….so what business do you have with us? We're still in mourning if you haven't noticed," Kam says, cutting to the chase.

"Looks more like still in training to me. There's no right way to get revenge, but there is a smart way. Wade used to talk about his brothers in arms nonstop, I'm just here to do what I can to help push you forward in the right direction," Frank states.

"In other words…?" Jace presses him to continue.

"In other words, I'm carrying out a promise made a long time ago, so let's see what you two got," Frank insists. He walks ahead of the two and swings open the double doors, inviting himself in. The inside of the building is a far cry from the dead land surrounding the outside. It had been completely refurbished into a Japanese-style space with green padded squares lining the floors. Along the walls are dozens of various weapons, with three rooms all labeled for a specific purpose. The new space was a mirror image of their last dojo, except for a large mural painted along the furthermost wall. There the three wise men can be seen on camelback gazing up at the stars as they anticipate the birth of a miracle. Upon entering Frank, Jace, and Kam all just so happen to gravitate towards the breathtaking mural, fixing their gaze upon the large quote below perfectly placed for those to see.

"The man who has it all fears all. The man who has nothing fears nothing," Frank reads aloud. "Beautifully said, but let's get to work. So Kam, Wade told me you were proficient in hand to hand combat and swordplay. I also heard that Jace was proficient in Taekwondo and melee, with weapon mastery as well. I wanna put all that to the test right here," Frank states as we takes off his jacket.

"And how are you gonna do that?" Jace asks with a furrowed brow. Frank then waves his hand, motioning him into the center of the dojo. "Are you serious? Alright, just remember you asked for this," Jace chuckles to himself before running at Frank full speed. He quickly feints before throwing an overhand right, but his arm is immediately caught and he's Judo flipped onto his back with ease. Frank looks down at him with a condescending smirk, which sends Jace into a fit of rage.

"Never take your opponent lightly. That's rule number one," Frank states. Jace suddenly flips up, holding two scimitar swords in his hands. The uncharacteristically crazed look in his eyes causes Kam to intervene before any blood was shed.

"Relax brother," he says, placing a hand on his shoulder. Regaining his sense of self, Jace flips the swords around in his hands a few times before they miraculously disappear. "I learned that from a magic show by the way," he jokes, now with the usual goofy smile on his face.

"Jace, I see you pulled two weapons out of thin air, good. That means Wade's death wasn't the only life-changing event you two had. I'm assuming Kam can now manipulate shadows then, is that correct?" Frank asks. Staring off into space, Kam suddenly flicks his wrist, inviting a pool of darkness into the room.

Looking down at the smoky haze rolling in like fog, Jace responds saying, "Well there's your answer."

"Even if you switched powers, the facts still remain the same. Kam, you need to learn how to use your powers as an extension of your body and stop running away from it. Jace, you need to reign in your emotions on the battlefield and actually learn the full extent of your abilities. Now knowing what I have to offer, riddle me this. What are you hoping to accomplish from training?" he asks after scoping out their strengths and weaknesses.

"I'm gonna find them and I'm gonna end them. Simple as that," Kam asserts with conviction.

"Simple as that," Jace nods in agreement.

"There's nothing wrong with your conviction, but make sure you never lose your sense of self in the process," Frank warns them. Jace slowly nods upon hearing this while Kam continues to stare into space with his hands in his pockets. When all is said and done, the three begin their intensive training. A few weeks into their new lifestyle, the relationship between Frank, Jace, and Kam begin to noticeably flourish. In the middle of the dojo sitting in seiza is Frank and Jace diligently cleaning their katanas.

"I appreciate everything you've done for us these past couple of weeks. I been studying like hell in the library just so I can perfect this weapon. It's just a little larger than a .50 cal. It's custom made for a special type of bullet with a thicker barrel and larger cylinder to absorb the recoil. There's enough explosive power to blast a hole through an elephant the size of a frisbee. Not to mention a gas-operated reloading system and textured finger locator. Figured it'll be better than that Glock 22 on your hip," Jace states.

"Gift giving? What do I look like, one of your call girls?" Frank asks.

"What you just say to me?" Jace snaps, now gripping the gun a little tighter.

"Calm down, it was just a joke. I humbly accept your gift," he replies, extending his hand and bowing his head.

"Is it me, or does Kam seem to spend a lot his days in there?" Frank suddenly asks, pointing towards the meditation chamber.

"He has been seeming real zen lately, maybe he's perfecting his craft like I was. I know I been practically living in the room next door, but we really haven't talked much recently," Jace responds with a shoulder shrug. Finally bringing their sabbatical to an end, the two men decide to spend some time at home for a change. Though the house was full once again, the atmosphere seemed all but empty. The only thing left to fill the air was tension. Sitting alone in the living room couch is Mrs. Holland, who had been washing down her dinner with a glass of wine. She notices Kam walking to the fridge and immediately invites him over.

"Oh, it's my little Kameron! Your attendance has been spotty lately, hun; don't tell me you've been avoiding us? At the least you usually pop in here and there, is everything okay?" she asks.

"Yes, ma'am. I've just been training," Kam replies.

"Well anyway our favorite soap is on; why don't you sit down and watch with me for old time's sake? I think Sebastian's finally gonna propose tonight!" she says excitedly, patting the sofa cushion.

"Nah, I think I'm just gonna lay down," he nonchalantly replies.

"Aw, come on, humor me for a bit, you're still my little Kam after all," she pleads. Kam starts to take a step forward but pauses upon seeing his dear little brother making his way through the kitchen. Large bags can be seen under his eyes, and his usual slicked back sandy blonde hair is now unkempt.

"Joe!" Kam excitedly blurts out. With a blank expression on his face, he walks past the two, completely ignoring their presence.

"He still needs time," Mrs. Holland comments. Kam starts to head back to his room but suddenly turns back around upon hearing a familiar voice coming from the TV.

"I'm Alexander Hamilton, no relation, and I implore you to vote for me if you want to see a real change in the acting government of today. We no longer need founding fathers to drive our society. We need creators. We need innovators. We need heroes," a sharply dressed Caucasian man states while standing at a podium.

"Isn't that the guy Wade wants in office?" Kam asks following the commercial.

"It sure is. I'm not supposed to say anything, but in honor of Wade, we took some initiative and offered to fund his campaign for Governor. We firmly believe he's the change Pearl's Gate and every other city needs," Mrs. Holland discloses.

"If only Wade was alive to see it," Kam snarls while clenching his fist. As he walks off, every single light in the house begins to ominously flicker, from the porch all the way to the pool.

"Tell me you seen that, too, Dad?" Jace asks before taking a seat in his father's study.   "Of course I seen it. It's probably just something going on with the circuit breaker," Mr. Holland says in disregard.

"By the way, how's Joe doing?" Jace asks.

"Not so hot. He stopped going to baseball practice and eventually started missing games, too. Recently he's just been holed up in his room. He needs a good old-fashioned boys night if you ask me," Mr. Holland insists.

"I'm probably the last person he wants to see. Just tell him I asked about him, okay?" Jace urges.

"Tell him yourself. Maybe he can talk you out of wearing all that jewelry. What's with the gold chains and watches lately? You haven't been snooping around in my safe, have you?" Mr. Holland jokingly asks.

"What, these? I'm just tryna make use of this new power to be honest. Kam might not need a way to cope, but I do," Jace replies with a shoulder shrug.

"And what makes you think he doesn't?" Mr. Holland suddenly asks.

"I don't know he just always seemed so strong to me, ya know? I don't usually hold anybody in high regard, but that inner strength he always had was something I used to look up to. Come to think of it, I only really seen him cry once. It was the day of our parents' wake, everybody was smothering us with hugs and offering their condolences. In the middle of the room, shining brighter than anyone else, was Kam just smiling away while giving thanks. Meanwhile I couldn't look anybody in the eyes without completely falling apart. About an hour in, I ended up running upstairs to hide, that's where I heard a noise coming from the bathroom. There he was crying his eyes out, no sign of the brave face he had been putting on all day," Jace tells him. Mr. Holland then rises from his seat and leaves him with some food for thought.

"And how can you be so sure things have changed since then? Hiding emotions, not speaking, he's probably more hurt than you know…" As Mr. Holland makes his exit, Jace decides to pick up the phone and call Kam.

"Let me just make sure…" he mumbles to himself. Their conversation goes as follows:

"Yo, where you at?"

"I'm in my room, what's up, you tryna train?"

"Nah, I'm just making sure you're okay"

"Yeah, I'm good, are you good? Like, why would you even ask that?"

"Forget it, bro. I feel stupid for even asking.."

"I guess…" *click

After their meaningless exchange ends, Jace heads towards his room with a scowl. He ends up passing by Kam's room on the way and starts to slow down. He eventually comes to a complete stop and starts backtracking until he reaches his door. He doesn't even bother to knock but instead slowly pulls down the door handle and peeks his head in. What he sees next causes him to immediately shut the door. Surrounding a meditating Kam are half a dozen wraiths all hovering around him, humming a synchronized hymn. Jace is completely taken aback for not even he had seen anything like this before. Closing his eyes to dissolve the rising panic, he takes a deep breath before stepping in to intervene. By the time he opens the door again, the wraiths are all positioned directly behind Kam. Every single one of them is staring at Jace, who is now wielding a long katana. Shielding him from what they believed to be impending danger, the phantoms decide to wrap him up and carry him into the darkness. The sight of Kam suddenly being pulled into a sea of nothingness causes Jace to cry out loud.

"NO!" he bellows. Following this thunderous shout, both Mr. and Mrs. Holland dart up the stairs and burst into the room.

"What hell is going on?!" Mr. Holland asks.

"Kam, he…ah…they…wraith…" Jace tries to explain, but his words turn to mush.

"What is that?" Mrs. Holland asks, pointing at a small black vortex twirling around the carpet.

Coming to a realization, Jace suddenly mutters, "Maybe this was him leaving a trail for us to follow. This might be my only chance to bring him back." Jace walks up to the spinning vortex with a look of pure determination. He seemed to have found his resolve and was planning to fully delve into the abyss.

"Please be careful, Jason. Whatever you do, save him from himself," Mrs. Holland sniffles as Jace takes a leap of faith into the darkness.

"What? What's going on? I don't understand this feeling. It's like….it's like everything's alive. The voice in my head is screaming to go back. Why can't it stop screaming for help?! AH, shut up! Shut up! I can barely think!" Jace's strained voice echoes as he wonders into mystifying territory. He finds his mind descending into madness every passing second. He seems to be desperately trailing through a seemingly endless void of nothingness. Though there's just barely enough light to see what's directly ahead of him, this large pocket of space is almost pitch black. The longer he's in there, the more he feels like his head is gonna explode for there's an inexplicable feeling of mixed emotions scrambling his brain. A few minutes in, he finds Kam sitting there in the same position as if his mind had transcended past any world or realm. He was in a complete state of serenity oblivious to the chaos closing in on him.

"Kam! Kam!" he bellows out. What responds to his screams isn't Kam, however, but a towering beast daring to take the form of a dragon. Until now it had just been laying comfortably behind Kam, unbothered. The dragon raises its head, staring at Jace with its pupils dilated as if it's waiting for him to make a wrong move. Jace stands there with his chin now raised and chest puffed out in an attempt to match the mightiness of the beast before him. After a moment passes, the dragon lays his head back down, seeming disinterested.

"Listen, Kam, I don't think I can stay in here for too much longer. I just wanted to let you know that regardless of what you're going through, you never have to hide your pain from me. Trust is delicate because it's instinctual, you expect to trust family naturally, so when that trust is betrayed, it's hard to understand why. You deserve to be iffy about certain situations, but there's no situation where I would ever turn my back on you. I wanna be glad to have worked through this as a family, so let's…AH!" Jace just barely finishes his sentence before he starts to lose his mind. Gripping his head, he frantically rushes back towards the spot he came from before Kam's shadow realm causes any permanent damage. After hearing his brothers speech, Kam slowly begins to open his eyes. He rises up in a panic and follows Jace's path, but he finds the spot to be just as empty as everything else in this treacherous void. He lets out a small sigh as he turns around, holding back a stream of tears. All of a sudden, the face of his birth mother appears from the shadows calling out to him. She's standing directly in front of him with long, flowing black hair and an angelic smile. Seeing this completely sets his heart at ease in a mere instant. He tightly grips his chest as he lets all of his emotions pour on to the ground like a rain storm.

"Mom I…I couldn't save him. I couldn't save Dad, I couldn't save Wade…whose hero am I? Whose?!" he calls out while sobbing uncontrollably.

"It's okay, my little Kam. It's okay to be hurt. It's okay to be afraid," his mother responds reassuringly. Upon saying this, her voice, along with her presence, both begin to fade into the abyss. Kam desperately reaches his hand out in an attempt to bring her back to him. What he wanted more than anything in the world was to hear his mother's voice.

"Mom!" he screams with his hand reaching out. In turn a gentle hand finds his grasp and squeezes it tightly, pulling him close.

"It's okay to be afraid. It's okay to be afraid," Mrs. Holland repeatedly assures him as she tenderly holds his head in her warm embrace.

"Mom…" he mutters to himself, completely surrendering to his mother's loving touch. Now back into the real world, Kam realizes he can face it head on as long as he's got his family. A teary-eyed Jace and William Holland join the two for a long overdue family hug. Standing behind them in the open doorway was Joe, staring at his so-called family with a distasteful look. Before he takes his leave, he spits towards the ground and shakes his head.

"So are we gonna talk about the dragon or?" Jace jokingly asks with a hint of concern. "No."

Chapter 10: Second Act

With positive emotions running at an all-time high, there seems to be no place for malice to bear fruit. Like a snake shedding its skin, malevolence takes on a new form as it finds another target to sink its teeth into. Crossing into foreign territory in a blacked-out Bentley Mulsanne is none other than the nefarious duo Alias and John Doe. The dead silence filling the air has a certain hint of danger, for one can only imagine what type of wicked intentions flood their minds. The first to break the silence is John Doe.

"Your power to give and take has proven quite useful I must say. To think my minions could receive grace as well..." he praises.

"Yes, it certainly is fascinating. However, the fact that only the bodies of your fallen comrades seem to be able to handle the power is worth thinking over. The corpses must require a unique genetic makeup to withstand my power," Alias states while treating herself to a complimentary glass of champagne.

"Hmm, could it be that the trials weren't as much of a failure as I initially thought?" John starts to think to himself. "I agree that there has to be some sort of catalyst for the abilities to synchronize with the body. For me it's all the more reason to act with a sense of urgency," John states. "Speaking of which, how are you adjusting to your newly acquired powers?" he asks. "Adjusting? There's no need for that. Even if the power is stolen by my hands, it just feels just like another extension of me. Every soul that I take is like a prophecy being fulfilled," Alias responds wearing a devilish grin.

"The sin of gluttony and the sin of wrath, you certainly are more of a force to be reckoned with than ever, my dear," John comments.

"Well hell hath no fury as they say. Though ironically enough this ability to manipulate ones memories seems to be the most useful of all. I'm glad we killed that one before he could pose a serious threat, but maybe I should've kept him alive as my little pet," she replies. She then looks into the rearview mirror, giving a small wave to the driver as she seductively licks her lips. The now blushing chauffeur slightly lowers the partition but is cut off by a finger wag from Alias.

"Ah, ah, ah," she whispers signaling for him to keep his eyes on the road. Her little teasing act is abruptly cut off by John Doe.

"By the way, what did you do to those two boys back there? From what I seen, foul play would be an understatement," he asks.

"Oh, just further testing my experiments. Though I doubt they'll even live to see tomorrow. They'd be lucky to even have a chance to say goodbye to their loved ones before they join their brother in the afterlife," Alias quips.

"And here I thought I was the only one with a flair for the dramatic," John replies, shaking his head.

"Was that a joke I just heard?" Alias asks in surprise.

"We're here," John announces as they pull up to a small video store about halfway through Ontario. From outside you could read "Video Geek" in large block letters atop the small building. On the inside is your typical hub of entertainment and nostalgia. DVDs, games, and other small merchandise line the store walls, and dozens of racks of films fill up the floor space. Though the place seemed like your average video rental shop, there seemed to be no customers in sight. Furthermore there was only one lone man sitting up at the front counter, though he wasn't quite dressed for the task. Laying back with his legs propped up on the counter was a distinguished man wearing a luxurious pea coat over a blazer with dark shades and a light stubble. If there was anything separating his appearance from that of a shady broker, it would be that he has a large silverback tattoo engraved on his neck. He seemed to have found the perfect read, for the look of irritation quickly spread across his face upon hearing the ringing of the welcome bells.

"We're closed," the man calls out with his wrinkled brow now grooved like a maze. "Arthur Prime. We've heard a lot about you, my friend," John Doe states.

"Yeah, well who hasn't?" he sarcastically asks. He's wearing a complicated expression, looking as if they had just told him the sky was blue.

"Hmph, funny, well we didn't come for an autograph. Show us where you keep the exclusive footage," Alias demands.

"I'm not sure what you mean by that," Prime replies, subtly slipping his gloves off.

"The fact that you've been assigned here is proof enough, so let's not play dumb. We know CORE labs has been tucking away their dirty little secrets in places like these," Alias states.

"Well that's news to me, I'm just filling in for the manager," Prime answers while slipping his shades into his coat pocket.

"I must admit, I'm a little relieved we get to do this the hard way, Mr. Prime. Alias …" John says, motioning her forward. Sliding two large icicles down her wrist, Alias moves in on the attack. She steps in for a double slice, but Prime had other plans. He quickly leaps up and hangs on to the ceiling lamp, greeting her chest with a powerful kick. The sheer force behind such a kick would've put a professional linebacker out for the rest of the season, but Alias merely stumbles back a few paces. She smiles a sinister smile as her body begins to rapidly flicker, and in the next moment, she disappears into thin air. Before you knew it, the air was wrapped up in an eerie stillness. Even the eye of the storm wouldn't dare blink in this foreboding atmosphere. The sound of tearing flesh suddenly breaks the silence as Arthur Prime is seen teeming with gashes from an intangible foe.

"What's the matter, Arthur, aren't you gonna transform?" Alias whispers from somewhere in the room. Prime claws at the air beside his ear in an attempt to catch her before she moves away. Growing beyond irritated, he crouches down as his bones vigorously twist and break. A long set of fangs protrude from his mouth as patches of hair grow around his face and from his knuckles. Shades of brown fur begin to grow from his entire body with a rounded muzzle and nostrils evolving along the upper surface of his face. His body drastically shrinks several inches going from 6'2" to 5'7" as he takes on the form of a macaque.

"Ah! Damn, why does it feel like the first time?!" he bellows out.

"That's a very naughty thing to say, Arthur," Alias calls out from the shadows.

"I may not be able to see you, but I can sense you!" Prime warns her while sniffing the air.

"We didn't have to take it this far ya know. It could've been as simple as you scratch my back, I scratch YOURS!" Alias yells out before she strikes. Anticipating her movements, Prime spins and grabs her arm before she can connect.

"Impressive…but not enough," John mutters as he watches Alias clutch Prime's throat in retaliation. She's grinning maniacally while slowly lifting him off the ground with one hand. Now suspending in the air, Prime's beady eyes begin to widen as his pupils constrict along with his windpipe. You can hear a slight sizzling sound on account of the heat starting to radiate all throughout her hands. Before he's burnt to a crisp, Prime begins to once again transform. The chilling sound of cracking and grinding bones fill the room in the act of Prime taking on a new simian form. Now with a shortened snout and elongated tail about four feet, he uses his neoteric Hyoid bone to let out a deafening shriek. Saved by the clamorous wail of his howler monkey form, he's quickly released from her grasp. The one screaming from shock wasn't Alias, however, but Arthur Prime himself, who seems to be in excruciating pain. He drops to the ground on one knee, wincing between shallow breaths.

"What's wrong, Arthur? Is the pain too much to bear?" Alias teases.

"It shouldn't feel like this. I don't understand what's going on…" Prime murmurs.

"Oh, you don't understand? Since the beginning, I've been lowering your pain threshold little by little. I would think twice about shapeshifting from now on, I mean it doesn't really seem to be your thing, am I right?" she says turning around, meeting John's gaze with a smirk. No response from John Doe, who continues to quietly observe the intriguing battle. He swiftly moves to the side to avoid Prime's elongated tail swinging by in retreat.

"Running away are we?" John asks the moment he passes by.

"Oh, Arthur, I expected so much better from you," Alias says shaking her head.

"What the hell?" Arthur starts to mumble to himself. His path had been abruptly cut off by three of John's loyal undead. All in sync, they pounce on Prime and hold him still with one on his back and two on his legs. They latch on to him with a deadly grip as though rigor mortis was still in effect. While kneeling on the ground, one zombie in particular starts to sink lower and lower down. Eventually the ground underneath them begins to crack as if this pile of skin and bones was suddenly the size of an African elephant. The overbearing weight of this decayed minion causes Prime to slam to the ground helpless. Once again his bones begin to break, but this time seems to be the act of someone else's will.

"AH! GOD!" he screams emphatically, completely ignoring Alias' dire warning to never transform again. He starts to miraculously grow from 5'7" to 6'5" in a mere matter of seconds. Silver fur springs from every part of his body, and his muscle mass seems to have quadrupled as his stature now mirrors that of a gargantuan Silverback Gorilla.

The skeleton that had been weighing him down prior to his transformation was instantly squashed beneath his feet like a grape. He grabs the other two and throws them back at Alias, who in turn incinerates them completely with a fireball.

"Easy now," John Doe warns her. Paying him no mind, she heads toward Prime to finish him off before he can put his overwhelming strength to use. She stops about six feet away and faces him, grinning ear to ear. Now on both knees panting like a dog is Prime, clasping his chest groaning in between breaths. He starts to mercilessly pound the ground in a fit of rage and frustration, but it only seems to further amuse Alias. She shoots an array of large icicles out of her wrist in an attempt to put him out of his misery. Prime quickly crosses his arms using his hulking forearms to block. By the time he brings down his guard, his legs are already wrapped around a pair of extended arms stretched like taffy. Alias effortlessly whips Prime around, throwing him head first into the back wall. In a cruel twist of fate, the gorilla-sized hole in the wall reveals the secret room he had been so desperately trying to protect.

"Hmph, turns out you can be useful after all," Alias scoffs while peering into the room full of secrets.

"Please…I don't know what you people are, but I'll tell you everything I know if you spare me. Please I have—"

"A daughter? Let's see…Mira was it?" Alias cuts him off before he could finish pleading. Prime raises his head in confusion upon hearing his late daughter's name.

"How did you…Mira?" he asks in utter shock. His face nearly matches his fur as the color flushes from his body. He reverts back to his human form and embraces his daughter with everything left in his heart. "Mira, I…I'm sorry," he starts to speak but can't seem to find enough words to match his emotions. All he can manage to do in this moment is pour his tears onto the floor while hugging his daughter tight.

The young girl leans in and whispers in his ear, "How could you put anyone before your own daughter?" Upon hearing this, Prime grabs her shoulders and pulls her away to look into her eyes as she continues to speak. "I'm dead because of the choice you made, and now so is Mom."

"What? How did you know about Kristen?" Prime asks, absolutely horrified. To add on to the hysteria, John Doe reaches down, smacking the ground. He rises up gripping a ginger surprise by the scalp. Surrendering to his grasp is a deteriorating woman in a nightgown with a large chunk of flesh hanging below her chin.

"No. No, no, no, no, oh God, Kristen…that can't be my angel…that can't be my angel…" Prime mutters through quivering lips. Looking him directly in the eyes, the woman begins to speak. John lends his voice as the words she speaks seems to be coming from both of their lips in a horrifying ventriloquist act.

They simultaneously recite Hebrews 11:6, "And without faith, it is impossible to please God." Prime drops back on his hands and scurries away in terror.

"Those were Mom's last words before she took her own life. She wrote them in her own blood to let you know you didn't only kill me but her beliefs as well," Mira says in a somber tone. To drive their point home, John Doe slices the woman's head clean off with one swipe. Little Mira grabs the dismembered head and places it next to the cowering Arthur Prime.

"All these years you've been wondering what you could've done differently. You made things more difficult than it had to be. The easiest choice would have been you, would it not?" John asserts as the two leave him to reflect on his own decisions. They then completely incinerate the video store with the scorching heat of Alias' flames in order to destroy the compromising files hidden deep inside.

"Wait, so you can kill off the zombies, but I can't?" Alias openly complains as they walk towards the car.

"If I give them life, it's only right that I'd be the one to take it away," John naturally answers. The unstoppable duo once again flee the scene victorious.

"So where does your story begin?" Frank asks all of a sudden.

"What, the first time I touched home plate?" Kam jokingly answers.

"Right, you mean the first time I hit second base?" Jace responds with a smirk.

"Alright, calm it down," Frank tells them. "I'm asking when all this Hero Trinity business began. When's the first time you really decided to go hard?" he asks, unknowingly adding fuel to the fire. Jace and Kam start rolling on the dojo floor laughing uncontrollably. About five minutes later, the laughing stops, and they both face Frank with an intense look on their faces.

"It's a beautiful story actually," Kam says as he begins to narrate. "So one day, Joe was getting his gut pushed in by four older kids, and we decided to step in. We were around thirteen around the time, so poor Joe was only about ten-years-old," Kam explains. After that Jace chimes in to continue.

"The other kids were about sixteen or seventeen, and they knew our family had money, so they decided to rob the weakest link. As they were reaching in his pockets, I just rushed in with a spear and knocked the wind straight out of the guy. After that Kam flew in with the BABOW!"

"You're not telling it right, bro. So yeah I came with a mean Superman punch and put buddy down quick. At this point, me and Jace are standing side by side looking like a two man army guarding Joe," Kam boasts.

"Facts, so next thing you know, all four of 'em are cracking their necks looking like they're ready to rumble. I might've told Kam 'that's our ass' or something like that cuz I knew it was over with," Jace continues.

"They were just starting to corner us in when a cool breeze blew in carrying Wade, who had an emotionless look on his face. He came charging in like a white knight and immediately flatlined one of the boys off rip. He was the most chiseled motherf–"

"You get the point…so basically it's three on three now, and we just knew we were bout to take the W with Wade there now," Jace cuts Kam off and takes over. "With the attention all on Wade, me and Kam both rocked the biggest one with a double whammy. After they seen their leader go down, they picked him up and ran home before they met the same fate. And that's how it happened," Jace concludes with a shrug.

With a look of profound confusion, Frank states the obvious and asks, "So where did the name come from? I get the hero act but…"

"You didn't let me get to the best part. After we knocked some teeth out, Joe was looking at us with sparkling eyes marveling at our bravery. He started praising us, screaming 'YEAH! You guys are like heroes! The Big Three, The Big Three!' At first that name almost stuck, but after some thought, we figured that it would sound better on somebody else. And that's how the Hero Trinity you know today came to be," Kam concludes. Slightly impressed Frank responds to their story with a nod and slow clap.

"That was some story, guys. Now that you've got your legs beneath you again, you can start looking to make a new name for yourselves," Frank encourages.

"That's a good idea. New chapter, new beginnings," Kam replies in agreement. They all join hands in unison to honor their vow.

"For Wade."

"For Wade."

"For Wade." Those two words were enough to shift the tide completely as the three men prepare to face their greatest challenge yet.

Chapter 11: Old Friend

Special Ops Base: Fifteen years ago

Standing proudly with their hands behind their backs and their heads held high are five of the greatest marksmen the world has ever seen. A few good men and a few fine women eagerly wait for their mission briefing. Their charismatic leader seems to match the title in every way, shape, and form; his commanding presence leaving the entire room frozen stiff and chilled to the bone.   "You might be the cream of the crop to the rest of the world, but you're nothing special to me. In my time, I've racked up 203 confirmed kills, and that's just the ones I'm allowed to tell you," their commander strongly states. One of the jarheads in the room can't help but snicker upon hearing what seemed to be nothing but a tall tale coming out of his mouth.

"I once seen him execute three men with a safety pin. Trust me when I say he was the one with the last laugh," a voice calls out from behind.

"The one who so rudely interrupted is Corporal Nina Monroe. She'll be stepping away from her current position to join the mission," the commander explains. Separating herself from the commander's shadow stood a pale young woman with a single blonde braid running down her back. She was short in stature, only about five-foot-one, but her attitude seem to compensate for what her body lacked.

"No need to explain to these pissants, Frank. They're not even w-"

"Hey, know yourself, Monroe," the Commander warns.

"Sir, yes, sir!" she salutes in correspondence.

"At ease," Frank responds.

"I'm sorry, Commander Bishop, but who is she to talk to us like that when I could easily snap her neck between my two fingers?" a brash remark comes from a brawny man at the end of the line. He's about six-foot-six with a hulking torso.

Veins are bulging from his arms to his forehead as he looks down at his comrade in utter annoyance. "This little girl gets demoted and prances around the room like she's worth a damn? With all due respect, Commander, it's laughable," the man continues. Noticing the blood dripping from Nina's palms that are now clenched in a death grip, Frank decides to step in.

"If that's what you truly believe, Sergeant Cavanaugh, then test your might," he waves his hand, inviting him forward. Suddenly everyone in the room steps back a few paces to prepare the arena.

"You sure you ready for this?" Nina asks, cracking her neck.

"I eat little blondes like you for brea–" BOOM! Before he could even finish his sentence, he's flipped on his back. The whole room is standing there in awe at the sight of this behemoth of a man laid down at the drop of a hat. Nina brazenly steps over the outstretched Cavanaugh but not before laying into his gut with the back of her heel.

"Pathetic," she mumbles to herself.

"Monroe! Get in formation!" Frank barks. "Any attack after the enemy is already defeated is overkill, you know that. Show me that you're meant for this. Show me that I didn't bring you along for no reason," he whispers to her, giving a sharp glare. He then proceeds to debrief the team on what's to come. "During these next few months, your life will be in my hands, so let's get this clear. I will never lead you astray, and you will never let me down. Most commanders will stand there and give you a long speech, but that's not me. We get in, we get out, and we go home. Now let's get to work." Two weeks later, the team arrives at their destination in South Sedan. They trot along the underground sewer system making their way straight into the villa of notorious warlord and child abductee Salim Otti.

"Livewire, set up base from here and shut down the whole security grid. Now's the time we split into our teams. With Echo running point, you three will head to the west entrance and clear it out. Thunderbird, Monroe and I will head south and take the bastard out before it gets too noisy. Remember, we get in, we get out, and we go home," Frank commands as his team heads out. They pop out of a manhole cover and immediately take out two guards, slitting their throats before they can even blink. Frank then peaks around the corner before signaling them to advance. With arrows sticking out of the chest of four wide-eyed guards, they zoom past the south wing with relative ease.

"Looks like I owe you one, Echo. Poor bastards didn't even see it coming,"

Frank whispers as they move along. They creep through the villa until finally reach a narrow hallway. At the end of the corridor, there's an exotic white tiger skin rug laid out on the floor in front of a curved white door. They all wait for Frank to give the signal, and with a nod, they charge through the door guns blazing. As soon as they bust in, they spot Salim taken completely by surprise, desperately attempting to grab an AK off the nearest table. Frank puts a silent bullet between his eyes before he even has the chance to fire. Just before they head out, they're stopped by Nina, who points at the bathroom door. The sound of a toilet flushing causes them all to raise their weapons, but what they see next is something they never accounted for.

"Ah!" A maid screams for her life as she's greeted by the barrel of several guns. She's pleading for life, shouting in Arabic while the team remains locked and loaded. Thunderbird and Monroe turn and look at their commander, whose eyes remain lost in thought for a brief moment. Nina takes matters into her own hands and mutters "no witnesses" before clutching the trigger. Frank quickly grabs her shoulders and stares into her eyes as if he's piercing into her soul. He then turns away with Thunderbird following his lead. The woman's quiet sobs are suddenly overlapped by a single gunshot. The maid's limp body falls onto the ground next to a sizzling shell as Nina stands before her once again muttering the words "no witnesses" as if to reassure her decision. They head back to the rendezvous point in complete silence.

"It was a tough call to make, Monroe. Either way something had to be done, so don't beat yourself up," Thunderbird speaks out.

"You gave the okay, right, Frank? Did I do the right thing?" Nina asks, staring into the back of Frank's head. Frank only keeps advancing, leaving her questions in the air. With her face increasingly growing distraught, she asks once again. "Frank. Did I or did I not make the right decision?" Her eyes rapidly dart back and forth with each word.

"There's Echo's team just up ahead. Let's prepare to head out," Frank candidly responds. As promised the team heads back home in one piece. Half a year later, they are once again called to action. In front of Commander Bishop is the usual ensemble of the five greatest marksmen in the world, but there seems to be a member missing from their ranks.

"Did Monroe go AWOL?" Thunderbird bluntly asks what everybody had been thinking. "Whatever the case may be, we have orders to fulfill. Let's focus on the task at hand," Frank replies. After being given their orders, the team is dismissed, and Frank is left alone with nothing but his thoughts. "I knew she wasn't meant for this…" Frank whispers to himself before he grabs his coat and leaves the room. Staring out of the car window reflecting on his past decisions is Frank, who snaps back to reality after finding his resolve. "This time I'll leave the blood stained on my hands alone," he says before grabbing his custom-made pistol. "What did Jace call this thing again? A 'Trinity Glock?' Damn, horrible name," he chuckles to himself before heading to the vantage point. The sinister Alias and John Doe have a surprise waiting at their doorstep.

"Achoo! Woo! Someone must be talking about me," Jace says, looking around the room. "Focus, bro, nobody's talking about you. We clearly need help if we're gonna find out where they're hiding," Kam retorts.

"What we NEED is for them to hurry up with our order. Had you not ordered the whole menu, we would've been out of here," Jace complains.

"Hey, I got expensive taste, man," Kam replies with a shrug.

"Pumpkin spice is not expensive taste," Jace snaps back. "By the way, bro, do you really think we can pull this off?" Jace asks.

"I mean we survived what she did to us and came out stronger than before, plus we have the element of surprise. They probably think we're dead, so we can take advantage of that," Kam answers.

"That's true, you got night vision and a dragon, and I got, well….you'll see. Either way we have no choice but to do this, or more innocent people are gonna suffer. This is for Joe," Jace says. They both look at each other in confidence.

"For Wade," the two say in unison.

"Order for Kam?!" the barista calls out. "And here's yours, sir," she says, discreetly slipping a piece of paper towards Jace while giving a seductive smile.

"I see you finally bagged one," Kam says with a condescending smirk.

"Yeah, but she didn't leave her name. Unless it's Jay's Laundromat, I don't see it on here," Jace says, continuously flipping the card around. "Wait, why does that name sound familiar?" Jace asks.

"Murphy's?"

"Hazel?" they blurt out two completely different answers.

"Wait what? What does she have to do with this?" Kam responds.

"Apparently it says she's the manager. Small world," Jace tells him.

"Doesn't this seem a little too convenient? I remember she told us she wouldn't be too far, but this is crazy. You think she knows anything?" Kam says thinking out loud.

"Well from what I seen in her eyes, she damn sure know something. Looks like we're headed to Jay's," Jace replies. What lies ahead is one of the many great mysteries yet to be unfolded. In the breaking hours of twilight, Kam and Jace approach the small white building with haste. The automatic doors welcome them in, and they're greeted by the staff almost immediately.

"Took you guys long enough. Good to see you holding up well, Kammie," Hazel calls out. She's standing at the back with her arms folded and brow raised.

"It's good to see you, too, Hazel," Kam responds.

"Uh, I'm here, too, you guys," Jace says, looking back and forth.

"Anyways follow me. I'm sure you wanna get down to business," she insists. They walk through the staff room door and enter a narrow hallway. At the end of the hall, there's a small door that looks to be nothing more than a storage closet. Hazel pulls out an old-fashioned skeleton key and turns the lock. They enter an unnaturally large room full of what can only be described as wonders. Dozens of large shelves fill the room with weird little knicks and knacks placed at every turn. Mountains of books are piled up in the far corner next to a large golden chest with several locks keeping it secure. There's various jars placed at random places, but they're all covered by cloths. Dead in the center of the space, there's a gargantuan golden chalice about twelve feet high, resting under a Persian rug riddled with elephant print. She starts to monologue as soon as they enter the mysterious space.

"Careful, don't step on anything. This library is my sanctuary, so trust me when I say there's a method to this madness. Excuse the archaic design, but you can have a seat right there, that's my main desk. Boy, don't open that shelf!"

"Sorry I thought I seen something moving in there. All things considered, this study is pretty fascinating. I would love to come back here sometime," Jace replies.

"I'll…have to think about that," Hazel responds hesitantly. "Now that the formalities are out the way, there's some things I been waiting to tell you. To a certain extent, I've been keeping track of what's been going on in your lives these past couples of months so you don't have to explain anything you don't want to. I know the pain of loss and I never want any of us to feel that pain again, so it's crucial that you have each other's backs in the battle to come. I've seen the type of chaos you're up against, and at this point, I want to find them just as much as you do. I can't join the fight personally, but I can help find their location," Hazel explains.

"Thank you so much, sis, that's more than enough. We would never ask you to join in the fight," Kam responds, showing his gratitude. Her words seem to have the opposite effect on Jace, however.

"So if you knew what we were going through, why didn't you step in? Just sitting there watching isn't weird to you?" Jace snaps.

"He sort of has a point, there's been plenty of times where an extra pair of hands could have helped," Kam agrees. Suddenly an unexpected hand is placed on Jace's shoulder from behind.

"Swine, my brother?" a mysterious man calls out, offering a slice of pizza. A gray-haired man with long dreads tied in a head wrap cuts the tension with a generous offer. He's wearing a red turtleneck with a lion pendant hanging from his chest.

"What the hell? What type of motherf–" Jace starts to say, but Kam cuts him off.

"Whoa, slow down, brother. Look again," he warns. The glint in his eyes reveal a flash of fear as he says this. Jace decides to back down and properly assess the situation. The calm and jovial demeanor of this man seems to warrant a hint of danger unseen to the naked eye.

"Damn, you're right. He's definitely more dangerous than he looks. On top of that, I've never seen you so cautious about someone, so I'm slightly on edge, too," Jace says. Hazel then steps in and takes the opportunity to introduce them all.

"This is the famous Brother Jay. I trust him with my life," she assures.

"Nice to finally meet you, Kam and Jace. I just want to say if anybody appreciates the work you do, the community does. If I could clean up the city like you, I would, but these days I'm just on light duty," he praises.

"I can't tell you how glad I am to have us all acquainted," she says before getting down to business. "So how this spell works is I take a strand of both your DNA and it essentially helps me find the person you want to see most in your heart. Unfortunately it only works for the living, you can take my word on that," Hazel explains.

"Whoa, wait, what a spell? What in the voodoo?" Jace retorts.

"Precisely," Hazel responds. She grabs a map from Brother Jay and holds out her hand as the two brothers donate a piece of their hair for the sake of humanity. As she binds the strands of hair together, it starts to glow a hint of gold with the magic instantly taking effect. Suddenly the hair starts to stretch across the map like a ball of yarn as Hazel begins to speak in tongues. After it's done winding its way around the map, the hair incinerates, miraculously revealing a burning path straight to the heart of the enemy.

"1425 Cherry Street. They must be hiding in the abandoned museum down there. They lost funding halfway through, and it's just been sitting there ever since," Hazel discloses.

"That's only a few hours away. I damn sure wish we had a plan though," Jace comments. "Well, whatever you two decide to do, I wish you the best of luck. You say you want to see this place again, right? Come back in one piece, and you just might," Hazel states. They say their goodbyes and head for the door but is stopped by Brother Jay on their way out.

"I know you're about to face some formidable opponents, but the true enemy is the darkness inside yourselves. The only way to overcome that obstacle is to step through each door with four feet," he says, leaving them with a peace of wisdom.

"I understand," they both reply.

"Oh, that reminds me!" Jace loudly blurts out. Just before they exit, Jace walks up to Hazel with a parting gift. He pulls out a small box and opens it, revealing a lovely elephant charm with small emeralds decorated around it. "I remember what you showed me last time and I thought it was beautiful. I tried to replicate that beauty as much as I could, but honestly this pales in comparison," Jace says with a slight grin.

"So you do have good taste. But rest assured, there's more to this beauty than meets the eye," she warns them. As she says this, the room starts to quake and fill with a dazzling green light. The aura starts to manifest into the shape of an elephant as tusks once again take form around Hazel's face. Her eyes glow green as she bows in an introductory pose. This new entity can only be described as divine. The two return the greeting and finally take their leave before their own eyes get lost in the elegance. Roosting on top of a building approximately 1.5 kilometers away from the abandoned museum is Frank Bishop. He sets up his vantage point and adjusts his sights one last time before taking aim. He catches a glimpse of a provocative Asian woman in a skintight catsuit leaving the building accompanied by a group of men and women. "Damn. She's out of range. Let me take the shot before he decides to leave, too," Frank whispers to himself. He focuses on a single target sitting on a large throne. The hooded man has his hand rested on his chin, watching as dozens of his subordinates sluggishly drag their bodies around the room like drug addicts. Frank takes a deep breath and slightly squeezes the trigger but is abruptly brought to a halt. He sees a small zombie-like figure limping towards John Doe on command.

"I-I know that outfit. Blonde hair tied to the back? No….no, it can't be. Please don't let it be her," Frank pleads. The woman turns around and stands at attention directly in front of John. John rises and stands before her with his hands pressed on her shoulders. He ominously stares out of the window, fixing his gaze exactly 1.5 kilometers far.

"She must've went AWOL and decided to volunteer for the experiments. Did I push her to do this? I'm truly sorry, Nina. This kind of life….you weren't meant for this," Frank thinks to himself, making up his mind to seal two fates in one shot. He takes a deep breath and pulls the trigger. Just like Nina so proudly boasted about in the past, Frank performs yet another incredible feat as the bullet zips straight through the inside of a fallen letter "e" that had been hanging in front of the window. Crashing through the glass, the bullet manages to blow a large chunk off of Nina's skull and leave a gaping hole in John Doe's chest in a single shot.

"Kill confirmed," Frank says through gritted teeth. He packs up and heads back home, wishing the final words said to his protege had left a sweeter taste.

Chapter 12: One Last Dance

"Unfortunately it's gonna take more than that to kill me. Right…..Alias?" John says. Creeping from the shadows like a red widow, Alias appears from behind to spin the final thread around John Doe. "The biggest fault in having power is the illusion that it is absolute. I suppose those words weren't just directed to those young vigilantes, were they?" John Doe asks with a side eye.

"You knew our dance couldn't last forever, John. As a friend, I feel like there's only one thing I can truly do for you. We plundered through countless pyramids, tombs, national libraries, mausoleums, and lost cities and yet we found nothing. There's no way to bring you fully back to life, so why go through the trouble of building an army of the dead if you weren't fully committed to resting in peace yourself?" Alias replies.

"Truth be told, from the first day we met, I already decided my fate was in your hands. Over these last few years, I realized that I've been feeling more alive than I ever truly will. If this is where our paths diverge, then do what you must to continue the path to salvation," John says, peering into the darkness. He walks away from the throne, bows his head, and bends the knee to Alias.

"This mission was never gonna have a happy ending. I'll handle the dirty work on my own from now on," she says.

Alias then gives him one last tap on the shoulder before slicing his head clean off with her bare hand. As soon as John's head hits the floor, his whole army composed of about sixty undead soldiers gather around his corpse. Giving him the ultimate send off, they encircle his body and hold his head up to the sky like an offering. They slowly descend back into the earth in unison, giving Death the last laugh in their final tug of war with life. Alias approaches her new throne with only her most trusted subordinates at her side.

"Number One! Number Two!" she calls out.

"Yes, ma'am!" two suited men respond. Alias let's out a loud whistle, and suddenly two hooded figures emerge from the depths below. Kneeling gracefully in front their leader are two men whose bodies are no stranger to decay. One appears with a gas mask over his face, and the other seems to be a copy and paste of another man. His face is stitched all over as if it can peel off at any moment. They look no different from the rest of John's old minions, except for one slight change.

"At your service ,ma'am," they both call out in a raspy tone of voice.

"As you can see, gentlemen, these two were part of the special project John and I had been working on. Let's just say a few pieces of their vitality are still intact," Alias says. She crosses her legs while grinning ear to ear, seeming to have a newfound sense of fulfillment. "Now the real fun can begin," she snickers.

"If you're looking to throw a party, maybe it should've been a masquerade. I don't know what's going on with y'all, but damn, y'all ugly!" a voice exclaims from above.

"At least this guy gets it," a second voice chimes in, pointing at Alias' masked minion. Perched atop the railings of the museum building is the world's newest dynamic duo, sporting a whole new look. The first to make his debut appearance is Jace. As soon as he jumps down, a silver eagle crashes through the building and swoops in under his feet. Majestically gliding downward, Jace hops off the creature, wearing the most dignified face he can muster. His new red and gold armor resembles that of a samurai, with a golden wolf mask covering the lower half of his face. Number One suddenly steps forward and claps his hands together, sending a shock wave straight towards Jace. Jace guards his face with his forearm, easily tanking the surprise attack.

"This isn't your typical material, my friend. I mixed components from the strongest minerals in the world to make these suits," he boasts.

"Stand down, Number One. Let them finish," Alias commands. She then waves her hand at Kam, motioning him to come down.

"Think you can show me up, Jace? Alright, watch this," Kam mutters to himself. He kicks off the railing, performing a double back flip, and crashes to the ground, making a small crater with his fist. As soon as he lands, a large cloud of dark smoke bursts throughout the room like a magic show. As Kam slowly rises to his feet, all the smoke in the room is pulled in towards his body until only he is encapsulated in a dark aura. The darkness seeping from his body seems to compliment his new appearance. He's wearing an armored ninja suit with carefully crafted metal guards on his forearms and shins. The lower half of his face is covered by a scaled dragon mask with a pair of long fangs protruding from both the top and bottom row of teeth. Standing beside him looking far from impressed is Jace, who's wearing a twisted frown on his face.

"Really? The superhero landing? That's what we doing?" he sarcastically asks.

"Well don't you two look handsome in your new outfits," Alias interrupts, smiling a wicked smile. Her face seems to be cheery as ever, but a keen eye can sense the insatiable bloodlust oozing from her body.

"This is the only time I'm gonna make this easy for you. Just come in quietly," Kam demands. Upon hearing those words, an ominous scowl suddenly washes over Alias' face.

"You think you're the ones going easy? You're only alive because I willed it so. I knew that if anybody, you two would be the ones to survive another awakening. Don't forget when I slit your little blonde cheerleader's throat, I stole his powers, too. I know more about your lives than you can possibly fathom," Alias retorts.

"Then you should've known better than to leave us alive," Kam snaps. Jace is too enraged by Alias's sharp tongue to wait for an answer, quickly chucking a spear straight through the chest of one of her minions. The minion cocks his peeled face to the side in confusion, but before he gets a chance to pull it out, the spear is ripped from his chest and returned to Jace's hand. Kam watches the whole exchange as Jace decides to finally wage war on Alias. As his eyes follow the returning spear, his view is suddenly obscured by the masked minion who managed to close the distance between them in a mere second. He knocks Kam back, connecting with his forearms as he managed to block at the last second. Large claw marks slightly burn through his armor guards, radiating what looks to be a lethal toxin. At this point, Kam and Jace have picked their opponents, but this fight was always meant to be handicapped. Number One and Number Two immediately join the fray.

"I guess I might as well even the odds a little bit," Kam says. A thunderous roar echoes through the room as the dark aura around his body shoots from his back and manifests into a malignant creature only few have seen the likes of. A black humanoid dragon rises from the depths of its own realm and greets Number One with a cloud of dark smoke. It blows its fumes around the two of them until they are engulfed in a sphere of darkness.

"What the hell was that?" Number Two exclaims. Watching the fight from her new throne, Alias sits with her legs crossed, seeming intrigued. Suddenly a small pillar shoots from underneath Number Two's feet, tossing him into the air where he's met with a devastating tornado kick from Jace.

"That was pretty cute," a voice calls out from behind Jace. Before he has a chance to fully turn around, another Number Two knocks the wind out of his chest, sending him flying back.

"If you can barely handle two of us, I'm scared to see what four of us will do to you," he boasts as his body miraculously splits into three separate entities. Right on cue, the man with the mismatched face steps in holding five fingers up in correction. Jace keeps his composure as him and Kam now stand back to back, ready to face the odds as a team.

"You have fun with that," Kam jokingly whispers to Jace. However, his actions speak differently as he attempts to turn around to help Jace but is blindsided by a booming kick from the gas-masked goon. "Alright, now you only got one more time to do some B.S. like that again," Kam angrily warns while flipping back on his feet. From the darkness, he pulls out two black Dao swords custom made by Jace, with a dragon emblem on each hilt. Suddenly the masked minion spits out a dangerous green mist before Kam can advance. Kam responds by ripping through the air in a spinning motion, his sword creating a dark current strong enough to send his poisonous spit back towards him. Small traces of ash run along each blade as Kam continues his assault. A few feet away, clones are being thrown at Jace left and right. Two clones use their combined strength to propel the third one forward at the speed of a bullet. Jace counters by throwing out three batons, hitting their targets with deadly precision. As the batons bounce off their skulls, they reconnect in mid-air and are pulled back into Jace's grasp, forming a long staff. The man with the sewed-on face suddenly makes his move. He breaks the pillar to pieces with one shot and sends a large chunk flying at Jace. In a flash, a metal blade protrudes from the end of Jace's staff forming a glaive, in which he attempts to slice the debris in half with. To his surprise, the large chunk of rock phases straight through his weapon, and he is instead greeted by Number Two and his clones. Face, chest, legs, and ribs, Jace faces a barrage of devastating blows that send him flying.

"Damn, these bastards are better than I thought, but every power has a weakness. No matter how many clones he makes, essentially I'm only fighting one person. I just need to find the real one and mark him somehow. Cut off the head and watch the body squirm, right?" Jace strategizes to himself while wiping the blood from his mouth. Before he can get back on his feet, he feels a major draft pass by his cheek. Carved into the wall is the gas masked minion who Kam sent crashing into the concrete with authority. The goon immediately pops back out, cracking his neck and straightening his posture. Kam looks down at his withered swords and starts thinking out loud.

"They're taking a lot of damage, plus it looks like he's getting serious. I should play a little more defense until I see the full range of his powers. Same height, same build, this should be interesting," he mutters. Kam then returns one of his swords to the shadows as he takes an animalistic fighting stance. With eyes like a hawk and feet like a feather, he faces his opponent with deadly intent. With an unorthodox stance of his own, the masked man cocks his head back lets out a loud roar. The mist rains down on his face, slowly burning his mask, only to reveal smoky blue eyes that look eerily unhinged. He opens his mouth only to reveal small fangs seeping venom like a viper. Before the last drop of spit could hit the ground, the man strikes at lightning speed. Kam returns the blow but not without consequence, taking a few claws to the chest. The masked man looks down at his hand, and to his surprise, it's disintegrating by the second. Small traces of black smoke can be seen eating away at his fingertips, but he quickly severs his fingers before the darkness can spread. He snaps his head up at Kam, who can't help but smirk at the sight of it all. Running along his blade is a smoky haze, his sword seemingly dancing with the dark.

"See now I'm not the only one playing keep away," Kam says, shrugging his shoulders. "FINISH THEM!" Alias angrily shouts. Not long after she snaps, the shadow dragon reappears, tumbling across the floor. Number One walks out of the dome with a smug look on his face. He then sends a deafening sonic boom at the shadow dragon who had been crawling towards Kam in retreat. The dragon is blown back towards Kam's chest, but he immediately absorbs it into his body before they can clash. Now merged as one, Kam takes on a miraculous transformation as black wings sprout from his back and small horns extend from his head. He soars into the air hovering directly over Number One and lets out a fiery blast, spewing a miasma of dark haze straight at him. Number One retaliates with a massive concussion wave dialed to eleven. The two clash with compelling force in an almighty power struggle.

"Ah!" Kam screams as he pushes back with all his power. His shadow flames finally start to overwhelm Number One, who's slowly evaporating before their eyes. Suddenly the masked goon attempts to blindside Kam as he finishes off his target. Before the goon gets a chance to make his move, however, a tomahawk slices through the air, taking his hand clean off as Jace jumps in to cover his brother's back. Leaving his guard wide open, the man with the stitched face rushes at him full force. Jace bends his body back to dodge, but the goon counters with a sweep kick. While on the floor, Jace attempts to throw a capoeira kick from the ground, but he goes right through his body. The goon then stomps at Jace's stomach, but a spike pops out from his armor and digs into the goon's foot. Right on cue, Kam swoops in with an earth-shaking roundhouse kick.

"Where was that when I was fighting, like, ten people?!" Jace complains.

"The cavalry comes when you need it most," Kam boasts. The two once again join forces as they continue to clear the gauntlet and face the final boss.

Chapter 13: Revelations

"Time to show you guys why I'm a three-time champion," Kam says while sending his second sword back to the shadows and putting up his guard.

"Not against Wade you're not," Jace immediately quips.

"Combat hat trick is all imma say," Kam replies as he takes a few steps back.

"Winning three separate martial arts titles isn't a flex, let it go," Jace fires back. "By the way, watch your step," he warns. All of a sudden Kam is springboarded by a pillar straight into the stitched man. With an ultra-sharp focus, he starts to send a barrage of blows at him in a frenzy. Rapidly losing ground, it seems Kam has left him too vulnerable to remain in his tangible form. The peeled face corpse decides to take a huge leap backwards in retreat. Just as Kam is about to follow his lead, he sees a long pair of claws phase through the man's body in a sneak attack.

"No more surprises," Kam mutters as he forcefully grabs his partner's arm and hip tosses him to the ground, leaving a small crater. The masked creature tries to spray Kam from below, but his field of vision is quite literally cut off. With a running start, Jace makes his football debut sending a booming kick before he can reach Kam with his deadly mist. The sheer power from the kick nearly leaves his head knocked loose as it's now hanging from his shoulders like a marionette. His acid rain abruptly shoots to the side, hitting Number Two right in the leg. As he drops to his knees in pain, all of the clones follow suit giving away his advantage.

"Now we'll always know where the real one is," Jace says to Kam, who nods in agreement. Kam suddenly flies in the air, spinning, the wind beneath his wings causing a powerful current. He violently crashes down on one knee, closing the curtains on the puppet show. He leaves no possible way of return as the corpse's head dramatically glides across the floor. Jace grabs the little hairs the head has left and tosses it at Alias's feet. Glaring at the severed head, Alias rises to her feet and ruthlessly crushes it with her heel.

"Pathetic," she says before folding her arms in an imposing stance. With half the pawns left on the battlefield, the remaining two decide to choose their opponents in a one on one.   "Looks like you get to take Number Two-Tone over there, I'll handle rag doll," Kam jests. With this the final battle continues. Kam rushes the rag doll in an attempt to blitz him before he can react, but he already expected as much. As Kam slips through his body, his shoulders are grabbed and he's slammed through the wall. Before the rag doll can finish the job, Kam is already back on his feet. With his back against the wall, his movements are restricted and he barely has time to block the incoming punch. To his surprise, the rag doll fist goes right through his head, and instead he uses the momentum from his feint to throw a spinning back kick. Mid-way through the kick, his leg is grabbed and he's instantly clocked with a devastating overhand right from Kam. Kam follows up by coming down with a powerful knife-hand strike but his hand is grabbed.

"Got ya," Kam says as he quickly closes his fist, slamming into his chest with a one-inch punch. A split-second before the punch can completely knock him back, the rag doll connects with a crushing knee to the body. "To be honest, if we're gonna keep going blow for blow, I don't see myself losing," Kam sneers.

"Am I seriously losing right now?!" Jace exclaims as he's seemingly overwhelmed by his four opponents. As they advance, two clones cross back and forth in order to enable confusion. As they break off to the side, only one remains in his sight.

"Where's the last one?" Jace thinks to himself. Suddenly a clone springs into the air as they all attack at once. With his staff in hand, he leaps into air and sends one flying back in two strikes. As he comes down, he slams his staff into the ground with a sound like cracking thunder. This causes a ripple in the ground around them in which the clones are all juggled into the air. Jace finishes off by using his staff to swing around and knock two clones into each other with a running kick. Leaving his back exposed, he's met with a flying knee dead in the center of his spine. Though his vertebrae is sent into shock, Jace finds the strength to grab Number Two's neck from behind and slams him into the ground with his favorite wrestling move.

"The devil's in the details, you can't hide that leg from me, bud," Jace says as he finds the one pulling the strings. A collar suddenly appears around Number Two's neck as he's now bound by chains. Following this a bed of spikes slowly emerge from the far wall. Jace then uses his full strength to whirl him around in one full swing to gain momentum. With his feet frantically scuffling on the ground like a cockroach with its head cut off, Number Two claws and tugs at his neck in a desperate attempt to escape his fate. Jace releases the chains from his hand, and he's sent gliding towards the bed of spikes. Now back on their feet, the clones are madly running in single file, all sharing the same thought. They're hoping to grab the chain in time to save themselves, but instead they're welcomed by a large harpoon straight through each of their skulls. Instantly the clones fold into each other like an accordion as Jace shatters their collective consciousness in more ways than one. With another piece cleared off the board, Alias has no choice but to enter the battlefield. Kam quickly intervenes in an attempt to put an end to it before it begins. He rises into the air and once again shoots his black dragon's breath at Alias. She merely extends her hand, absorbing the full force of the blast with relative ease. She then extends her other hand and aims it at an unsuspecting Jace. A brigade of boulder-sized fireballs shoot directly in his path as she uses Kam's power to amplify her own. Bombarded by the first two blasts, Jace barely manages to create a heat shield before he's turned to ash. Watching his brother desperately struggle to shield himself from the heat, Kam decides to cease fire. He pants heavily while descending down as he realizes the heavy burden of this attack. Before he can let out another shaky breath, his throat is nearly crushed by Alias's elongated arm, which miraculously reaches his neck from several yards away.

"Listen closely, baby, never reveal your trump card to the best player in the game," Alias whispers. She then slings him to the ground so hard, the room slightly shakes. Bound by a sudden gravitational force, Kam finds it impossible to move.

"What the…what type of move is this?!" Kam gripes. Alias then looks towards her rag doll and gives him a quick nod. Understanding the assignment, the rag doll heads toward Kam to put him out of his misery. As expected his path is cut off halfway by Jace, who sends him crashing into the wall with his shield, forcibly sandwiching him between the two. He follows up by calling upon his silver eagle, which rips through the air, aiming straight at Alias's head. Sensing its presence, she immediately turns around and grabs it by the wings. Even the strongest of men can barely manage to bend an iron bar, but Alias's astronomical strength exceeds that of any mortal man. Easier than ripping up a bad essay, she tears its metal wings apart with her bare hands. All the while Kam uses this distraction to stagger back up on his feet. Once again he summons his shadow beast on a call to action.

"I just need a little time," he tells it. Jace catches on and creates two large silver Dire Wolves to accompany the beast. Kam turns to Jace and starts to point to various spots in the room.

While chuckling Jace shakes his head and says, "I guess some superhero landings are worth a damn. So what do you need me to do?" They barely manage to wrap things up before two severed wolf heads come sliding at their feet.

"Return!" Kam calls to his dragon. The mighty beast flies directly into his chest on command. "Job well done, buddy, I couldn't have asked for a better partner," Kam whispers. Jace immediately turns to him with his face contorted, silently mouthing the word "what?" in confusion.

"Oh, my darlings, I'm sure you'll have plenty of time to talk in hell," Alias says as she approaches. She suddenly stops in her tracks and slams her foot on the ground, causing a small tremor. Before they realize it's a diversion, the rag doll is halfway to Jace's back with one of his metal spikes in hand. At the last second, Jace springs in the air with a backflip, simultaneously shooting a stone golem from the wall. The golem glides along the floor with its fist up like a battering ram. The loud snapping of bones echo through the room as the rag doll slams into Alias at an alarming speed. She catches his limp body and violently tosses him to the side. In that same moment, Jace throws three golden tridents up in the air and kicks each one in a separate direction. Just a few yards shy of their target, the tridents all suddenly vanish. Before her rag doll can make his next move, a trident instantly torpedoes through his chin from a smoky portal below. His mummified body drops down to the floor, leaving his head on a spike like a trophy. Before Alias has time to react, the remaining two tridents are firing in opposite directions, aiming directly for her head. She easily deflects them but not before being ambushed in an aerial assault. Kam is crashing down with his sword, looking to cut her down in one blow. She quickly looks up and blocks his sword with her forearm. Jace steps in with a spinning back fist, but his wrist is caught with her other hand.

"All out of op—" she attempts to say, but her airflow is abruptly cut off. Through the shadows, Kam's second Dao sword pierces straight through her lung. He then jumps back in retreat, successfully falling through with his plan. Leaving his brother to finish her off, he watches as Jace opens his hand and extends a large spike from his wrist.

"Remember this?!" Jace angrily shouts as his weapon starts to sink into her neck. Before it can deal any lethal damage, Alias grabs the spike and forcibly snaps it off of his wrist. She then hurls it at Kam like a kunai. Kam had immediately blocked the spike with his sword, but it left him with no time to react to the incoming bloody blade that she uses to rip through his shoulder.

"Blood for blood. An eye for an eye," Alias says with a derange glare. With Kam now impaled by his own blade, he drops to the ground in shock. Jace takes initiative and grabs both of her arms, holding her still. He then starts to encase her arms in gravel, taking away her greatest asset before her eyes. Seemingly unfazed she jumps up and digs into his chest with a drop kick. After pulling the sword from his shoulder, Kam tosses it aside and rushes at Alias. Two shadow hands rise from the ground and grab her feet, buying him time to close in. She shoots a fireball downward, causing the shadows to disperse. Through the fire comes a flaming side kick from Kam. She responds with a devastating right to Kam's shoulder as the two dig into each other's wounds with a crushing blow. Kam rolls to the ground while Alias slightly winces from the pain in her side.

"Not so fast," Alias says as she punches an incoming stone golem so hard, the gravel around her arms crumbles. She then slams her other fist into the ground, breaking both hands free. She suddenly turns to Jace, grinning ear to ear with a bloody smile.

"You know it's funny, Jason, you're out here struggling for your life while your worthless father is out there struggling with his sanity. Two Collins boys, and neither of you parasites have the strength to fend for themselves," she taunts. Jace hangs his head down and falls silent for a few seconds. He crashes to his knees with a huge thud.

"Just as I thought," she scoffs. As he's caught in a trance, larges vines start to slither along the ground and wrap themselves around his hands in restraint. One slides up his back and loops around his neck. Alias slowly walks up, wearing her most wicked grin to boot. She grabs his long hair and snaps his head back so she can look into his eyes. Surprisingly enough Jace is returning her gaze with a malicious grin of his own as he inconspicuously shoots something towards Kam like a pool cue.

"NOW!" Jace shouts as he watches Kam launch her minion's dismembered hand into her back, filling her body deadly toxins. Alias yells while snatching the zombified hand from her back. Jace forcibly breaks free from her vines but not before a large pillar of ice tears off a chunk of his side in retaliation.

"AH!" Jace howls in pain. Everything in his mind suddenly went blank, and for a brief moment, he felt like he had been pricked by a thousand needles and dipped in dry ice. An excruciating pain shot through his body, sending him into instant shock.

"JACE!" Kam loudly screams. With movement transcending the speed of lightning, Kam instantly closes the distance in a single strike. His eyes are fluctuating between light and darkness as ominous shadows dance around the ember gleam. Before her body can fathom the pain of her organs bursting, Alias stares at the hand running through her stomach. Forcing a recovery, Jace breaks off pieces of ice from the pillar and launches it into both of her legs. He staggers up while holding his side but uncovers it just in time for Alias to see metal glimmering from where his fatal wound used to be. Though she was dropped to her knees a moment earlier, she once again rises up from the ground, only this time against her will. With his hand crushing her throat, Jace suspends her in the air as he slowly begins to turn her body into stone.

"WAIT!" she shouts before she's completely solidified. "With wounds like these, there's no way I'm coming back from this. At least let me die like royalty," she mutters while nodding towards the throne. Obeying her final wishes, Kam and Jace carry her to the throne and slam her into the seat. She glances back and forth between the two with a look never seen before. The type of look a mother makes when she's gazing upon her newborn child. The look of pure satisfaction, the heavy sigh of relief.

"If I can teach you anything about this world, it's that there's always a bigger fish. Evil takes on many faces…..but how do you question evil if it's wearing the face a God? The sins of the father, the death of the man, the shame of the woman, there's meaning to it all. Your parents' death…..was no accident," she uncovers. Hearing those words suddenly seemed to strengthen the intensity in their eyes. "Look at me how you wish, as cliché as it sounds, there's no pretty way to expose the truth. The government, the hospitals, the schools, the C.OR.E. runs it all. HE runs it all. If you're man enough to bring me down, then you better become twice the man you are now to take on what's next. After you discover the truth for yourselves, only then will you finally heed my words, ONLY THEN will you start to take on my will," Alias boldly affirms. "My fearless knight," she says, brushing Kam's cheek. "My apex predator," she calls out to Jace while stroking his face as well. They both stare into her eyes with burning fire. They can't help but ponder whether they can trust any of her final words. However, her very last word seems to shake them down to their very core.

"AWAKEN," she commands as she draws her last breath. Suddenly the room starts to violently quake as the brothers are once again put through the wringer. They grip their skulls, writhing in agony and frustration. They desperately look to the sky as an inexplicable energy courses through their veins like a defibrillator. This time instead of thrashing around on the ground, they are both struggling to stand on their feet as they fight the unbearable pain. By the time they come back to their senses, they notice a subtle change in the atmosphere. They look around the room and watch as each of the scattered bodies are being pulled into the depths by dozens of decaying arms. Carefully examining his body, Kam notices something strange.

"Whoa, my wounds stopped bleeding," he discovers. "What about you, bro?" he asks Jace.

"Nah, I definitely feel everything," Jace responds while looking down at his metal side. Something happens to catch his eye as he's looking over his body. "Huh? What's this?" he says before picking up a singed ID card from the floor. "Hey, isn't this ole' buddy?" Jace asks. Glancing over Kam responds with, "It looks like him, but the names scratched out, that's weird. I guess John Doe is all he'll ever be."

"Oh well. Let's get out of here and let Frank know we're alive," Jace says as they head out of the building. They can't help but turn around and look at Alias one last time before they head out.

"Let's just leave her sitting on her throne like a true queen," Kam chuckles.

"Facts. I don't know if that last speech was an attempt at redemption, but she's definitely still going to hell," Jace snickers. With the battle coming to a shocking end, it seems all of the sins of the past have been washed down into the next generation. Once again the thread of fate seems to have brought the two men to a place close to their heart.

"Geez, you boys look like hell," Murphy says with a concerned expression.

"Don't even ask, Murph," Kam replies with a tired sigh.

"Psh, have I ever? Looking at your outfits, I'll just chalk this up as one of those, um…what you call 'em, cosplays or something like that," he concludes.

"Well if you like Prime, then you'll love these guys," Kam jokes while pointing between him and Jace's outfit.

"Oh, speaking of which, didn't Jace tell ya? Ever since the big man himself came through, business has been booming! I even scored a picture! I may even blow it up and put it on the front window, what do ya think, huh?" Murphy rambles.

"Yeah, yeah, yeah, can we just use your phone? I know you practically live here, so spare us a change of clothes, too, if you can, good sir," Jace cuts the chase.

"Yeah, sure thing, but spare me with the good sir B.S. I ain't too old to put a foot in your ass. Anyways I should have a few extra shirts in the back. Follow me, fellas," Murphy immediately replies. As they walk to the back, Kam seems to have come to a realization.

"Yo, Jace, doesn't it bother you not knowing what she did to us? I'm tired of being put through these circumstances where all we can do is pray that the good outweighs the bad," he suddenly says. Reading the room, Murphy heads back to the front of the store after opening the closet door.

"To be completely honest, there's been so many things going on back to back that's been killing me inside. I don't think I can handle another so called 'awakening,' man," Jace solemnly replies.

"Even though you say that it's still undeniable that we come back stronger every time. I know one thing for sure though, because of us, Wade can finally rest in peace," Kam assures, his smile giving off a hint of uncertainty. After a quick of change of clothes, they finally give Frank a call.

"Yo, Frank! It's ya boys! Huh? What you mean who's this?! Come on now, you know who this is, stop playin'! So yeah, apparently we fought the good fight and survived but like literally, just barely. Except for Kam, who must've took a booster shot or something cuz he looks healthier than a Russian race horse right now. No but seriously listen…" Jace's voice trails off as Kam heads to the front of the store shaking his head. He quickly finds himself glued to the TV where a familiar face steps up to a podium to give his speech. As Jace finally makes his way to the front, he's immediately tapped on the chest by Kam, who guides his eyes to the screen.

"Isn't that Wade's hero?" he asks.

"Really? That's the guy he wouldn't shut up about? Chiseled chin, blonde hair, he looks like the world's richest frat boy," Jace sneers. The two can't help but cackle while watching the campaign speech.

"I'm Alexander Hamilton, no relation, and I've gathered the entire city here today with one thing in mind: hope. Sapphire City has birthed so many remarkable and award-worthy innovators in a short span, but somehow we seemed to have forgotten where our roots came from. Julius Scott and Chanelle Collins, two of the greatest minds I've ever had the pleasure of working with. Where are their statues? Where are their plaques? How can we remember greatness if their legacy has nothing to stand on? That's why during my campaign, I will be partnering with C.O.R.E Labs to fund the Pathogenic Particle Packer research project. Try saying that three times fast, right? This facility will be made in memoriam to continue Dr. Collin's and Dr. Scott's extraordinary work on Epidemiology. That's not all, however, it is with great honor that I can announce that the renowned Holland family has donated a whopping $1 million to this project, not to mention an extra million to be dispersed to children's homes all throughout the country. Speaking of which, I myself will be personally reaching out to the children of Julius Scott and Chanelle Collins to offer them their own share of the company. Kameron and Jason, I hope you guys are watching. I'll be seeing you soon." Alexander Hamilton's gaze seems to shoot straight through the screen piercing their souls.

"Did we really just get name dropped?" Jace says, staring at the TV in shock. Sharing the same sentiment, Kam responds with a nod while staring in deep thought at the banner directly behind Hamilton. In that exact moment is when Kam and Jace suddenly seem to come to terms with the phrase "keep your enemies closer," realizing a new chess match has already begun. They synchronously speak the name out loud as if to invoke their presence.

"Huh, Creators Overseeing…"

"Revolutionary Experimentation."

The C.O.R.E. will continue…..